WEL

In spring, the ro... ...by trees of pale-gr... ...it becomes a leafy ... ...un splashes, winding its way towards the village. Along the coast, overhanging trees tilt above the sea and ancient roots swirl in the incoming tide. These tangled woodlands are all that is left of a vast forest land that was once called Trá na Coille.

In those far-off days, it was a wild, lonely place. Families fished along its coast. Farmers cleared the land and built their settlements from the strong oak wood. In medieval times, King Henry II granted the forests and a royal title to an officer from Bristol, James Hobourne. A castle was built and trees were felled to create a rich, pastoral estate for Lord and Lady Hobourne.

As the centuries passed, Trá na Coille became Beachwood. The trees continued to be felled, their strong timbers furnishing fine houses and mighty warships. Its population farmed and fished and traded, or they worked on the Hobourne estate which was located to the north of Dublin city. In 1970, the Hobourne family sold their lands and home to the Irish Government. Hobourne House became the local secondary school. Land was sold for development and housing estates were built with names like Oaktree, Cypress, Elmgrove and Ashwood. The gardens and grounds were turned into a public park. The population grew, and in Hobourne Park, young people began to gather in Fountain Square.

Today it is their favourite meeting spot. Ask them about Beachwood and they will tell you that it is a magic place with the sea and the city and the country all rolled up together. But during the winter months, when the trees form a bleak guard-of-honour and the grey sea lashes the coast, they will complain that it is Drearsville, on the edge of nowhere. I would like to introduce you to these young people as they move through the seasons. Join them on their good days and their bad days. Dance and play, fight, grieve, love and laugh with them. But most of all, enjoy them.

BEACHWOOD

THE SLUMBER PARTY

JUNE CONSIDINE

POOLBEG

First published 1993 by
Poolbeg Press Ltd
Knocksedan House,
Swords, Co Dublin, Ireland

© June Considine 1993

The moral right of the author has been asserted.

A catalogue record for this book is available from the British Library.

ISBN 1 85371 184 5

Cover design by Pomphrey Associates
Cover illustration by Brian Caffrey
Set by Mac Book Limited in Stone 9.5/13
Printed by Cox & Wyman,
Reading, Berks

Cast of Characters

Young People

Caro Kane

Susan Kane, elder sister

Jonathan Kane and Danny Kane, Caro's elder brothers
                (Danny is younger than Jonathan)

Jennifer Hilliard ⎫
Emma Patton   ⎬ Caro's friends
Aoife Johnston ⎭

Michael and David Hilliard, twins, brothers of Jennifer

Sonia Hanson ⎫
Greg Power   ⎬ Classmates of
Paul Johnston ⎭   Susan Kane

Keith Butler

Adults

Stella Kane, mother

Kevin Kane, father

Sergeant Hilliard, Jennifer's father, nicknamed
                        "Passion Killer"

Garda O'Hara

Patrick the Pizza Prince

Mrs O'Neill, Dekko Unlimited Video Shop

Loaf, bouncer at disco

Members of Celtic Seekers After Psychic Knowledge

Mrs Miranda Boggan

Professor Price

Locations

Oaktree Avenue

Oaktree Drive

Oaktree Crescent

Oaktree Green, play area

Hobourne Park

Twist and Shake

The Slopes

Magpie Cave

Shale Head

Beachwood Strand

Bowman's Lane and Spirit's Rest, where Mrs Boggan
lives

Pizza Palace

Sherbet Alley

Dekko Unlimited

Strand Shopping Mall

High Strand Street

To my nieces, Clare and Fiona Bolger

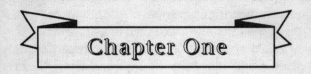

Chapter One

Mrs Kane often declared that the only good thing about a slumber party was that for one blissful hour before it started, she could look into her daughter's bedroom without suffering from heart failure. Last month, in desperation, she had hung a sign on the outside of Caroline's door. It read

This Room Is a Health Hazard. Enter at Your Own Risk.

But that notice, along with the jumble of clothes, books, records, board games with missing pieces, shoes, paint easel, sketch pads, dried-out paint pots and equally dried-out cereal bowls, coffee mugs, and rubber skeleton, had disappeared.

Caroline Kane (known as Caro to her friends) was small for her age, which was almost fourteen. She had black hair, cut below her ears, a thick fringe, strong dark eyebrows and blue eyes. When she looked around her tidy bedroom, she sighed with the satisfaction of one who has worked long and hard, which indeed she had. Knowing that as soon as her friends arrived, it would take only five minutes to return her room to its normal squalor, she breathed in the lavender scent of polish and enjoyed the sight of her gleaming dressing-table. Rows of tiny green frog figures stood to attention on top of her bookcase, pouting expressions of astonishment on their faces as she carefully dusted each one of them.

Her older sister, Susan, came in to inspect the tidy bedroom and stared around in amazement. "I never knew your carpet was that colour. Come to think of it, I never even knew you had a carpet."

"Ha Ha," said Caro, fluffing up her duvet.

"You kids!" Susan shook her head with adult wisdom. "When I was your age a slumber party meant one friend only—and lights off at midnight. As for watching videos and ordering pizzas and going to discos beforehand...you kids don't know how lucky you are."

"We kids do," retorted Caro, smugly. "Anyway, what are you moaning about? You're going to your beach party."

"I'm seventeen," said Susan. "I've earned the right to enjoy myself." She was convinced that the new generation of teenagers was spoiled rotten. Whenever Caro complained that she was the most bullied and exploited young person in Beachwood, Susan soon put her right on the subject. "You think you're deprived? I was fifteen before I could persuade Mam to let me go to my first disco and you were allowed go when you were thirteen! It was my suffering that made things easy for you." The same moan was heard every time Caro appeared in a new pair of jeans. "Mam would have freaked if I'd asked for 501s when I was your age. As for Converse! No way. St Bernard runners. That was all I ever got."

Not that Caro believed her sister for one moment. Susan had a brilliant social life—beach parties and sitting around the Rock Garden Café and drinking coffee until all hours with her friends in the kitchen.

Caro thought it must be wonderful to be seventeen. But being almost fourteen was not bad either. Soon her friends would call and the evening would begin. First they would pay a visit to Beachwood Village and stock up for the slumber party. Then they would get ready for the disco that was being held that night in the Beachwood Community Centre. At eleven-thirty, they would be collected and driven home by Jonathan, Caro's older brother, and the slumber party would begin. After laying down certain ground rules that her daughter promised earnestly to obey, Mrs Kane was allowing them to stay downstairs and watch a video after they came back from the disco. She had even agreed to pizzas being delivered to the house at one in the morning. Mrs Kane was an understanding woman. But, when it came to slumber parties, she had learned the value of taking certain precautions.

The ground rules were as follows:

1. Caro and her friends must not put on the Jane Fonda work-out video and do aerobics at any stage during the party.
2. They must not play the piano. This had happened on a previous occasion, sending Mr Kane hot-foot down the stairs at 3a.m. to restore order, which he did rather loudly and rudely.
3. They must sweep all popcorn from the floor, gather up all sweet papers, wash all glasses and put the lemonade bottles into the bottle-bank box in the back garden.
4. If they did insist on making pancakes, they had to wash away all batter, butter and sugar marks from the kitchen counter, walls and cooker.

5. They must not, under any circumstances, leave the house at any stage after their return from the disco.

This last demand was made in the firmest possible tones. Mrs Kane stared sternly at her daughter. "Do you understand me, Caroline?"

Caro was astonished and hurt that her mother could even think of, let alone suggest, such a possibility. But she understood her anxiety.

There had been big trouble on Oaktree Avenue when Aideen O'Connor held a slumber party to celebrate her fifteenth birthday. When the rest of her family were fast asleep, Aideen quietly left the house with her three friends and met her boyfriend, Rory. He was also having a slumber party with his friends in a tent in his back garden. Not that Rory called it a slumber party. It was a camp-out. By torch light, the girls had crowded into the four-man tent, giggling and nudging each other. They crawled over the boys' heads, generally getting the tent into the most appalling tangle. Then, just when they had settled down to share a bottle of Coke, the tent collapsed. Rory's father woke and looked out the back window in time to see numerous bodies crawling out from under the canvas. He knew his son hung around with a weirdly-dressed bunch of boys but, adjusting his eyes to the glow of thighs in the moonlight, he did not believe that any of them wore mini-skirts or neon-coloured leggings.

The after-effects had been dreadful. All the parents on Oaktree Estate cast suspicious glances at their sons and daughters. They began a third-degree questioning session about slumber parties, sleep-ins, camp-outs, over-nighters.

"Call them what you like!" said the anxious mothers and fathers. "Did you stay where you were supposed to stay? Or did you go off making mischief in the middle of the night?"

None of the adults would reveal what this mischief was supposed to be. Their children, having a pretty good idea of what was on their parents' minds, were none too keen on discussing it either. Aideen O'Connor's mother threatened to write to Gay Byrne and ask him to discuss "teenage slumber parties" on his morning radio programme. The teenagers groaned, loudly. They would never forget the hassle they had to put up with when Gay Byrne's morning programme opened up the subject of deep kissing at teenage discos. It seemed to go on forever. Every morning. Shock. Horror. Outrage. Questions and more questions.

Even Mrs Kane, who normally stayed very calm in the midst of such media sex storms, finally asked her youngest daughter if she had ever indulged in "that kind of carry-on."

Caro did not bat an eyelid. "You must be joking," she replied, knowing that she had yet to be kissed, deeply or otherwise. "I gave up 'that kind of carry-on' when I was in fourth class!"

The deep kissing debate had resulted in the cancellation of the Beachwood Community Centre Disco for two months! But worst of all, it started Sergeant Hilliard off on his morality campaign.

Sergeant Hilliard ran Beachwood Garda Station. He was a tall, burly man with a craggy face and jutting eyebrows. As far as he was concerned, there was only one opinion that mattered. His own. And this opinion told him that the young population of Beachwood were like puppy dogs, unruly and disobedient, needing their noses firmly slapped until they learned to obey orders. Not that he slapped their noses. After listening to the deep kissing letters and phone calls that were aired on the radio every morning, he organised the Beachwood morality campaign. Every night a patrol car searched for parked cars among The Slopes at Beachwood Strand. This was a favourite place for couples to park when they were going together but steamy windows were no protection against the probing torches of the members of the night patrol, who became known as the passion killers.

"It's so undignified!" Susan had moaned after one such experience. "They're treating us like children. Mr Johnston lent Paul his car last night and a crowd of us drove out to Shale Head. We were just listening to music and having a bit of a laugh when that creep O'Hara starts waving his torch and asking to check Paul's driving licence."

"Garda O'Hara's OK," said Caro.

When she was in primary school, Garda O'Hara had visited her class and talked to them about drugs and being careful when approached by strangers and road safety. He laughed a lot and, unlike the sergeant, seemed to believe that having fun was part of being young and that teenagers were able to behave themselves without an eagle eye watching everything they did. She suspected that he also disliked the morality campaign. But he had to do what he was told, especially because Sergeant Hilliard sometimes went along on patrol to check that his orders were being carried out.

Sergeant Hilliard lived on Oaktree Drive, two roads away from Caro. Jennifer, his only daughter, was one of Caro's best friends and was coming to her slumber party. She had warned Caro that her father would ring Mrs Kane to check out what supervision there would be during the night.

Caro wiped an imaginary smear from her wardrobe door, then ran downstairs to answer the telephone. As she suspected, it was the sergeant.

"I hope you young people know how to behave yourselves," he barked. "None of this staying up until all hours, do you hear me now?"

"Yes, Sergeant Hilliard," she replied meekly, sticking out her tongue at the telephone before going into the kitchen to call her mother.

"You needn't worry, Sergeant." Caro could detect a hint of irritation in Mrs Kane's voice. Sergeant Hilliard always had that effect on people. "I am perfectly capable of looking after a group of young teenagers. Yes! They will be supervised at all times. Yes! They will also be collected from the disco by my eldest son Jonathan. Of course he has his tax and insurance in order. No! He certainly does not drink and drive! Goodbye, Sergeant Hilliard. I must rush. I'm sure there is something burning on my cooker."

She slammed down the phone and made a growling noise in her throat. "What a pompous man. How did he ever manage to have such a nice family? For heaven's sake, Caro, you lot had *better* behave yourselves tonight or I'll never hear the end of it."

The doorbell rang. Caro could see the shapes of her three friends, Emma Patton, Aoife Johnston and Jennifer, through the glass of the hall door. As usual, Jennifer's voice drowned out all other sounds. Tall and broad-shouldered, with a splash of freckles across her nose and a voice as powerful as a foghorn, she was, like her father, difficult to ignore.

"You'd shout too!" declared Jennifer, whenever her friends told her to put a plug between her lips, "if you had

7

to make yourself heard over the noise of five older brothers and the local sergeant!"

In his home on Oaktree Drive, the sergeant tried to keep his unruly family under control. When they were younger, he had used a whistle for this purpose. He would stand in his doorway and call them in from play. One blast meant homework had to be done. Two blasts meant meals were ready. Three blasts meant trouble. The order was obeyed instantly. Her friends were used to Jennifer dropping whatever she was doing and dashing home like a hare on the chase when the whistle shrilled. Yet she had a cheerful personality and, despite her father's strictness, had become wilder instead of more sensible since she started attending Beachwood Comprehensive. Caro grinned as her friend's laughter boomed. They would have to stuff her face with cushions in the small hours of the morning to prevent her waking up the entire Kane household.

Aoife Johnston, in denim jeans and a check shirt, had a book under her arm. Her sleeping gear hung over her shoulder. During the slumber party she would probably find a quiet corner, curl up away from the others and start to read. She had a vivid imagination and could usually be encouraged to make up the most hair-raising horror stories whenever the occasion demanded. She had promised to tell them a vicious ghost story in the small hours of the morning just before they went to sleep.

Emma Patton, the third member of the group, had cropped blonde hair and a slim athletic figure. She always wore tracksuits or jeans and baggy sweatshirts with sporty logos on the back. Her ambition was to be a runner like Sonia O'Sullivan.

The girls gasped with astonishment when they saw Caro's room.

"Sorry. Wrong house," said Emma, ducking out again in mock-amazement.

"Very funny." Caro gave her a shove back in and looked anxiously around. She hated the idea of destroying the pristine appearance of her room and immediately tidied their dumped sleeping bags into a neat bundle under her bed.

"Can we cope with this?" Jennifer wondered, as Caro hung up their jackets.

"Give her ten minutes," advised Aoife. "My mother goes the same way when she does a spring clean."

"Did you manage to get Susan's gear?" asked Jennifer, seating herself in front of the dressing-table mirror and examining her profile.

Caro lifted out a pair of leggings from her wardrobe. They looked as if they had been made from tinfoil with cutaway knees and a gap just below the bum line. A vest in faded black silk with criss-cross laces up the front was added to the leggings.

"Does Susan actually *wear* this stuff?" gasped Jennifer.

"No. She borrowed these from Andrea Stone. I think she was hoping to change her image. But she lost her nerve. What do you think?"

"It's ghastly enough to be perfect," said Jennifer. Her eyes glinted with mischief. Swiftly, she pulled off her T-shirt and jeans and slipped into the leggings and top. For half an hour, the girls worked hard at transforming her. Her blonde hair, normally swinging to her shoulders, was teased and swept up into a beehive. Her eyelids were shadowy green, her lips pouted with a gleaming coral lipstick. She wriggled her feet into a pair of high heels that had once belonged to Mrs Kane.

"You look brilliant!" declared Caro. The other two

agreed.

"The shoes are killing me. I'll never make it to the village in them." Jennifer winced and hobbled across the room. "Do you think I'll fool Mrs O'Neill?"

"Absolutely!" said Emma. "You'll pass for nineteen, at the very least."

Jennifer looked pleased. The girls were hiring a video for the slumber party and had decided on *Dealing with Grave Matters*, the latest over-18 horror film, reputed to be the most frightening and sexy horror film ever made. A must for horror buffs, even if they were under-age. At fourteen, and the tallest of the foursome, Jennifer had been chosen to try and hire it out.

Caro checked to see if her mother was around, anxious that she should not ask any awkward questions about Jennifer's changed appearance. She could still remember the uproar that had occurred when Mrs Kane came home unexpectedly one afternoon and found them watching *In Bed with Madonna*.

The coast was clear and they hurried out the front door. As they walked down Oaktree Avenue, Jennifer staggered a few times. "It's like walking on stilts," she moaned. But she managed to avoid turning her ankle or dislocating her hip and eventually the four girls arrived in Beachwood Village.

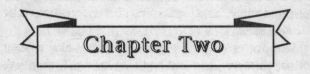

Chapter Two

At the Strand Shopping Mall, in the centre of the village, they stopped outside Dekko Unlimited, where Mrs O'Neill, the video librarian, was busily serving customers.

"Oh, I don't know..." Jennifer hesitated, hanging back from the doorway. "I don't think this will work."

"Yes, it will!" insisted Emma. "Go on. We'll wait here for you." She firmly pushed her through the entrance. Jennifer glared back at her friend, looking vulnerable as she stumbled on her too-large, too-high shoes. She scanned the shelves until she discovered the chosen film.

Outside the window she could see the others, their faces pressed against the glass. She ignored them and nonchalantly placed the video tape on the counter. Mrs O'Neill had eyes like laser beams and a voice just as sharp. She stared at Jennifer and shrilled, "Listen to me, you pre-teen squirt! Do you know that you can be charged with impersonating an adult?"

Everyone in the video shop heard her and began

spying between the video tape shelves at the unfortunate Jennifer, who was in danger of wobbling right off her shoes.

"But I'm eighteen," squeaked Jennifer. "On my last birthday."

"From the look of you I'd say that you've only just grown out of wearing Pampers," replied Mrs O'Neill. "Have you ever heard of a certain gentleman by the name of Sergeant Hilliard?"

"Never heard of him," squeaked Jennifer.

"We can soon fix *that*, young madam! If you don't leave that video tape back where you found it and select something a bit more suitable for your tender years, I'll ring him right now. I'm sure he'd be happy to discuss your age with you."

"Don't do that!" Jennifer, cheeks flaming through the blusher that Caro had applied so lavishly, selected *Child's Play 2* and wobbled out of the shop with as much dignity as the situation allowed. She was embraced by her friends who were weepy and weak with mirth.

"It was worth a try, if only for the laugh," declared Aoife, drying her eyes.

"Thanks a heap," howled Jennifer. "I could have been arrested for 'impersonating an adult' and all you can do is laugh. I could have been sent to jail by my own father! Bread and water and solitary confinement."

This made them laugh even louder. Eventually, as they walked up High Strand Street, Jennifer had to join in. They bought sweets and crisps in Sherbet Alley where Susan had been working full-time for the summer holidays. Finally, feeling very grown-up, they ordered pizzas, to be delivered from Pizza Palace.

"Hey Caro. I hope you ordered pizzas for us."

Caro's heart gave a little skip of excitement when she recognised the voice. She turned around and found herself facing Michael Hilliard and his brother, David. Jennifer's brothers were twins, double trouble, she always declared. As usual Caro could not make out whether the tall boy who spoke was Michael or David.

Jennifer had no such difficulty. "Butt out, Michael!" she ordered. "And leave us alone."

"Butt out yourself!" replied her brother, looking at his sister in amazement. "Since when did you decide to become a tart?"

She tossed her head and did not deign to answer him.

"Hey, Caro, I've a message from David, haven't I David?" Michael nudged his twin, who grinned, nodded and looked quickly away. "He wants to know if you're going to the disco tonight?"

"What if I am?" Caro replied, primly, hoping against hope that she wouldn't blush. "It's none of your business."

"I know it's none of my business," agreed Michael. The twins fell into step, one on each side of her. "But David would like to make it his business. Isn't that right, brother?"

"Don't mind him." David was beginning to look uncomfortable. He could hear Aoife and Emma giggling behind his back. "He's always messing."

"Me? Messing?" Michael was the picture of innocence. "You're the one who asked me to ask her if she was going!"

His twin brother silenced him with a rough punch on the shoulder and the two boys began to wrestle together.

"Yawn. Yawn," said Jennifer, patting her lip with her hand. "Why don't you children go home and play with your building bricks." She grabbed Caro's arm to steady herself. "They really are a pain. Just ignore them."

"I hear you girls are having a slumber party," said Michael, catching up with Caro. "How about inviting us back after the disco for some pizza? I've heard that mixed slumber parties are all the rage."

"I will not!" Caro was quite shocked. "It's girls only."

"Girls only." Michael whistled through his teeth and looked in despair at his twin. "That's sexist! Aoife, you're always going on about women's rights. Do something about this! Tell Caro to make it a mixed party. I'll supply the boys. We'll even bring our own pizzas."

Aoife began to whistle. David grinned and shrugged, as if to say, "Don't blame me. I had nothing to do with this."

Caro liked the Hilliard twins. But she had never paid them much attention until one night about a month ago when Michael tapped her elbow at the Beachwood disco and told her that David fancied her.

"He wants to know if you'll go with him?" he said.

"Go where?" Caro had asked, playing dumb until she got her mind back in order again.

Michael shrugged. "Go with him! You know what I mean. He asked me to ask you."

Boys always got their best friend to approach the girl they fancied and ask this question. It took away a lot of embarrassment, making it much easier to turn down the go-between if the girl was not interested. But Michael was so like David it was almost as if there was no go-between. Caro wanted to giggle wildly but had stared at the floor instead. Jennifer saw her confusion and told her brother not to be such a dork.

"Caro Kane has good taste. And it doesn't include you, goon-face, and your goon-faced shadow. She

14

wouldn't be seen dead with either of you!"

"I wouldn't go quite that far," Caro protested. But it was a silent protest. Truthfully, the Hilliard twins made her nervous. They were cool, so utterly alike, black hair, shaved high at the sides with long wispy pieces falling over their eyes. Their father moaned about rearing "nancy boys" for sons and Jennifer claimed that they lived in dread of him cutting off their fringes some night while they slept. But Jennifer also told dreadful stories about the tricks they played on other girls and on their teachers when they pretended to be each other. So, even if she fancied David, she would never dream of going with him because he was so like Michael and Michael was so like David. This whole thing of "going" with someone was confusing enough without the problem of trying to cope with an identity crisis. Michael had grinned, as if he knew exactly what she was thinking, and said, "If you change your mind, Caro, you know where to find me and the other goon-face."

Since then the twins had celebrated their fifteenth birthday and no further approach had been made, until now.

"Come on Caro. Be a sport. Invite us over. I like pizza. David likes you. We'll have a great time."

"No way!" She tried to march past him. But he dodged back and forth in front of her, blocking her way.

"Do you know that you can be charged with sexual harassment?" declared Aoife. "This is a prime example of male power control!"

"Right on, Aoife," said David, shouldering his brother off the pavement.

"Thanks a lot, pal!" Michael yelled. "I try and look after your interests and all you do is beat me up. Go and

15

get your own dates in future."

Caro was convinced that everyone in the village was watching them. Since the night of the go-between, she was beginning to notice certain differences between the twins. For one thing, David was a lot quieter than Michael, who was as brash and noisy as his sister. When he did speak, his voice was slightly deeper, his eyes were a stronger blue (or maybe that was because whenever she looked at him he was staring right back at her) and there was a tiny, almost invisible white scar on the edge of his lip. Jennifer said he had sliced his lip with the lid of a tin can when he was a baby. This made Caro quiver with sympathy. In fact, although she did not want to admit it, she was beginning to feel something quivery in her stomach every time she thought about David Hilliard. She was relieved when they rounded the corner into Bowman's Lane, a winding narrow lane that was also a shortcut to Oaktree Estate.

"Is this a private war or can anyone join in?" A voice spoke behind them.

"Hello, Mrs Boggan," they chorused.

An elderly woman was wheeling her bicycle, nervous of cycling over the uneven, pot-holed surface of Bowman's Lane. Her eyes widened when she saw Jennifer's clothes but she made no comment. David immediately offered to wheel the bike and Aoife linked Mrs Boggan as they made their way towards her bungalow. She lived at the end of the lane and her small bungalow, called Spirit's Rest, was almost hidden by overgrown bushes.

"Mrs Boggan, are you having a party tonight as well?" asked David when wine bottles clinked in the carrier basket as the bike wobbled over a pot-hole.

"No, it's not exactly a party, David." Mrs Boggan

could always tell the difference between the twins. "But I am entertaining a very important person, tonight. Professor Price, the President of the Celtic Seekers After Psychic Knowledge, is writing a book on Celtic folklore. He has heard about the ghost of Cross Hollow and is coming to Beachwood to do some research on our famous legend. What do you think about that?"

"Is he the Professor Price who wrote *Curves on a Ghost Graph*?" Aoife had become quite excited. "It was all about people who make money from fake ghosts and who make fools of the public and…"

"I know what it was about, my dear," Mrs Boggan interrupted her. "I helped Professor Price to compile many of those statistics."

"You helped write a *book*!" Aoife wanted to be an author when she grew up. "That's neat."

"There's no such thing as the ghost of Cross Hollow," said David.

"Maybe not," Mrs Boggan replied. "But the legend has lived on in this area since 1769, when the castle burned down, and that gives it some credibility."

Mrs Boggan lived on her own. After the death of her husband (he had been an extremely sensible man who scoffed at her claims of psychic powers), she had formed the Beachwood branch of the Celtic Seekers After Psychic Knowledge. They met once a month in Mrs Boggan's bungalow and had their annual Christmas party in a posh restaurant in the village called The Zany Crowe's Nest.

"What better place for a bunch of zanies," said Jennifer's father, who had no time for their strange notions of communicating with the dead and believing that even a caterpillar could be a human being, reincarnated. But everyone loved Mrs Boggan. She wore colourful long skirts, her hair was a fuzz of grey spiralling curls and she made her own earrings. She was also a palmist and was used to young people calling to her house in the hope that she would read love letters between the lines of their hands. Caro was thinking of paying her a visit and Jennifer had already called to her three times, intrigued by the letter T that kept appearing in her heart line. A new boy called Tom Parkinson had moved to Beachwood and she was convinced that he fancied her.

They stopped outside her gate. David wheeled the bike up the weedy driveway. The grass needed cutting and paint flaked on the window frames. "I'd ask you in but I've a meal to prepare," she said.

"That's OK," said Caro. "We're going to a disco tonight and I'm having a slumber party afterwards."

"How very exciting." The elderly woman smiled. "I'd better not delay you then."

"Ask her to invite us, Mrs Boggan," begged Michael. "Everyone has mixed slumber parties nowadays."

"A mixed slumber party. Now that would be really interesting. But somehow I don't think Caro's mother would approve."

"You can bet your sly buttons she wouldn't," cried Caro. David had returned. The way he kept looking at her made her feel really funny. "Come on you lot," she yelled at the girls, beginning to run in a sudden burst of energy. "We've got a slumber party to attend. And it's girls only!"

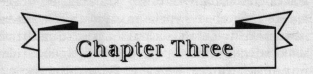

Chapter Three

W hen Susan opened her sister's bedroom door an hour later, she gave a yelp of astonishment. Four bodies lay on the floor, faces upturned, blind cucumber eyes staring at the ceiling.

"Don't make us laugh or our faces will crack," warned Emma, trying not to move her lips. The masks had been made from honey and oatmeal. Caro felt as if she had dipped her face into a cement mixer.

"Tickle, tickle, tickle." Susan walked between the four bodies. The cucumber eyes stayed closed. The faces remained rigid.

"Don't tickle me," pleaded Caro. "Just go away and leave us alone." Her voice sounded as if it were sliding through a tight letter-box. "We're getting ready for the disco."

Susan shaped her hands into talons and wriggled her fingers under Caro's neck. Sometimes, it was hard to believe that Susan was seventeen years old.

Caro spluttered with frustration. Pieces of oatmeal fell

on the floor. She knew exactly what Susan was doing, even if she could not see her. Although Susan's fingers did not touch her neck, tickling sensations rippled through her body. People only had to wriggle their fingers in front of Caro and her body went into a spasm. Once her father had tickled her foot and she had struggled so much that she kicked him in his right eye with her heel and left him with a black-purple bulge half-way down his cheek for a week.

"Tickle, tickle, tickle," whispered Susan, in a tickly voice.

"Ahh!" yelled Caro, yanking the cucumber slices from her eyes. "Go away!"

But Susan had moved to the far side of the room and was inspecting Jennifer's disguise, which lay in a heap on the floor.

"Don't tell me you wore that down to the village!" she exclaimed. "You could have been arrested for indecent exposure."

"I was almost arrested for impersonating an adult," said Jennifer. She managed to sound very proud of herself even though she was still talking through her teeth.

One by one the girls sat up. On their way out to the bathroom they left a trail of oatmeal across Caro's spotless carpet. Hair-dryers, tubes of face cream, ponytail scrunchies and a bottle of pimple-removing lotion lay on her bed. Like a fat worm, toothpaste eased out from an open tube on to the duvet cover. When they returned, faces pink and shining, Susan was studying the frog collection.

"Is anyone in your house going to this beach party tonight?" she asked Aoife.

"By anyone, do you mean my darling brother, Paul?" Aoife grinned.

"I was just wondering if he was working in McArthurs tonight."

"As far as I know he's not." Aoife inspected her face for stray blackheads. Susan seemed fascinated by the upturned faces of the frogs. The girls tried not to giggle and waited.

"Ahem...so...is he going?" The question was desperately casual.

"I think so. Not that he ever tells me anything. I'm just the kid sister."

A growl of agreement came from Caro.

Susan was hoping that Paul would ask her to go to the Beachwood Comprehensive Debs Ball. Caro and Aoife were working hard to make this happen but so far they had had no success. Caro liked Paul Johnston but she had to admit that he turned her confident, sensible, older sister into a witless fool even at the mention of his name. He was unaware that he had this effect on Susan and saw her as a friend, someone he could ring and talk to about his problems. A real pal. Susan sighed and sympathised with him, waited for his phone calls, drooped with misery when he didn't call and giggled through the top of her mouth in the most awful falsetto whenever he did. This sound normally caused Mrs Kane to roll her eyes heavenwards, clutch her hair in despair and mutter, "To think I was a card-carrying member of the feminist movement! Tell me, God, where did I go wrong with this daughter of mine?"

After Susan left, the girls changed their clothes for the disco. They admired each other, spun a few times in front of the mirror, caught Jennifer practising a pout when she thought they were not looking, and went downstairs.

21

"I was under the impression you girls were going to a disco tonight?" Mrs Kane stared at their tangled hairstyles, the torn knees and ragged hems on their jeans.

"We are!" Caro was disgusted.

"Sorry," apologised her mother, fingers itching to take out the sewing box. "You all look great. Have a smashing time and be ready when Jonathan comes to collect you. And remember, try not to sound too much like a herd of elephants when you come in."

By the time they arrived, the disco had started. Two bouncers in black tuxedos and dicky-bows checked their membership cards. They were big men with stern faces. If anyone caused trouble they moved in, fast. Two older boys were turned away at the door. They protested, shoved and cursed in slurred voices. The girls had seen them drinking cans of lager at the back of the community centre when they arrived. One of the bouncers held his arms out in front of them. His chest was the width of the two boys. Recognising this fact, they became silent and slunk away.

Sometimes, young people drank a few quick shots of vodka just before going into a disco. They figured that the bouncers would not be able to smell it on their breath. If it worked and they were able to stay sober until they hit the inside of the hall, the flashing lights, heat, loud music and crush of bodies normally knocked them out within a very short time. At her first disco Caro had seen a girl, who had been dancing wildly in front of her, suddenly slump to the floor and throw up before passing out. A bouncer had lifted her in his arms as if she was a feather. Caro had seen the look of disgust on his face, had seen how the crowd moved away and had felt ashamed, embarrassed for the girl who was so out of it that she would never have any memory of how slack-faced and limp she looked as she was carried through the crowd. But usually the bouncers at Beachwood Community Centre knew all the tricks and were quick to detect the slightest sign of alcohol on anyone.

"Come on, let's dance," said Emma, beginning to shake her head. They formed a circle, moving to the fast rapping beat.

"Hey, Caro, you look as if you have pimples all over your face," said Jennifer when the ultra-violet light came on and outlined her freckles.

"Thanks a lot," yelled Caro, arms waving.

The light turned their clothes brilliant blue-white and when the DJ pressed the flickering lights switch, their bodies seemed to shake in funny, jerky movements. Caro attended modern dance classes and had taught the girls special dance steps to do when this happened. It added to the weird, wonderful effect.

They stayed close together when the slow dances were on. Couples moved past, glued together by the heat and the crowd. Some couples kissed, an endless kiss that sometimes went on for the length of the slow set.

"Heavy stuff," said Jennifer, looking enviously at them.

"Hey look, Caro. There's David. I think he's looking for you."

Panic time! "Hide me," she wailed.

The girls formed a circle around her. Over Jennifer's shoulder, she watched the Hilliard twins. Two other boys were with them. David was scanning the crowd. He spotted Jennifer and began to push his way towards her. A couple danced past, lips together. Caro thought of the tiny white scar on David's lip and shivered. Suppose he tried to kiss her like that, in front of everyone? She would faint with embarrassment.

"Don't worry, we'll protect you," said Aoife. "We'll pretend you're not here."

The four boys approached. Three of them asked the three girls to dance.

"Thanks a heap," Caro hissed when her three friends headed for the floor, leaving her in full view of David.

"Would you like to dance with me?" he asked.

She wiped her hands on the side of her jeans, hoping he would not notice how sweaty they had become. He began to push through the crowd, leading the way, gripping her hand, tightly. They began to dance. He made no attempt to pull her close or to tighten his arms around her. Now that they were together, neither could think of anything to say. She realised that he was just as shy as she was. She linked her arms behind his neck. Their cheeks touched. Slowly they moved together and it seemed as if there was no one else on the crowded floor but the two of them.

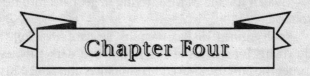

Chapter Four

An hour later and the girls were hot, sticky and breathless. Caro saw Keith Fowler coming towards her.

"Oh, I hate him! What'll I do if he asks me to dance?" she whispered to Jennifer.

"Tell him you will if he stops brushing his teeth with garlic juice," replied Jennifer.

"Brilliant," said Caro.

"Wanna dance?" asked Keith.

"OK," said Caro.

"Cluck, cluck, cluck!" said Jennifer.

Maybe she *was* a chicken. But Keith was in her year in school and she did not want to hurt his feelings. "What feelings?" Jennifer said afterwards, but it was too late by then.

In the centre of the floor, Keith was showing off. He fancied himself as a dancer and his idea of smart movements was to fling his body wildly in all directions. Caro saw David watching her from the side of the hall and did her modern dance routine. If Keith could show off, so could she. Keith bumped against her and almost knocked her over.

"Watch it!" she warned, trying to get back into her routine.

Keith grinned. His face was pink. Beads of sweat rolled down his forehead and his T-shirt had dark patches under the arm. He swayed his shoulders and flailed his arms, gone with the music. "Where did you learn to do that rubbish dancing?" he shouted and gripped her under her elbows. "I'll show you how to really move."

She tried to push him away but the crowd surged against them. He lifted her up and bounced her back on the floor.

"Leave me alone!" Caro was furious with him for making a fool of her in front of David. But he would not let her go. In school he behaved the same way, always creating trouble in class and doing his strong-man act. She managed to break free but she was caught off-balance and before she realised what had happened, she was sprawled on the floor, surrounded by a forest of legs. Once, she had gone with her father to see Ireland play an international match at Lansdowne Road and had experienced the same sense of panic when the crowd surged forward after Ireland scored a goal.

"Caro! Are you all right?" David had pushed through the crowd and was helping her to her feet. He swung around to face Keith. "Push off, Fowler, and leave her alone."

"She's dancing with me!" Keith scowled at him and shoved him out of the way. Once more, he threw himself into the music.

"Not any more, she isn't." David shoved him back

with his shoulder. A bouncer glanced fixedly in their direction. The two boys began to dance side by side. A war dance. They moved in time to the music as each tried to force the other out of his space. Caro was frightened by the glint in their eyes and their set expressions. She wanted to leave the floor but the crowd was dense and she could not see her friends.

The movements of the two boys were growing stronger, more determined, using their shoulders to nudge each other then drawing back in fluid, wavering movements. Keith staggered and regained his balance. "Stuff you!" His face darkened. He turned clumsily around and slammed his hand, palm up, into David's face. David staggered back, eyes stinging, then rushed towards him. Immediately both boys were grabbed by the crowd and forced apart.

"Hey...hey! Break it off," said a boy. "Do you want to be thrown out?"

"Let me at him!" yelled Keith, struggling wildly.

Everyone was watching them. Caro could never remember feeling so embarrassed. She wanted to burst into tears, hide in the darkness outside, run as far as she could from the two growling boys, who seemed to have totally forgotten about her. Then the bouncers arrived and everyone tried to act normal.

"Let's see your membership cards," they demanded, after separating the two boys from the crowd.

When Keith Fowler produced his card, the bouncer cut it in two with a small scissors that he took from his top pocket. Then he put the scissors and the pieces of card back into his pocket.

"OK! Start marching," he snapped.

David refused to hand over his card. He claimed to

have forgotten it. Caro knew that no one was admitted without it and figured that he was afraid they would find out his name. Sergeant Hilliard's son, fighting at the Beachwood disco! She could imagine what the bouncers would make of that piece of information. And what Sergeant Hilliard would do when he heard about it. When David continued to refuse to show his membership card, one of the bouncers lifted him up, until his legs were dangling in mid-air. The bouncer's hands reminded Caro of shovels digging into the soft flesh under the boy's shoulders.

"I'm a strong man," growled the bouncer. "And if I see your ugly face within a mile of this centre again, I'll personally see that you spend the rest of the night in a cosy cell, courtesy of Sergeant Hilliard. He doesn't take kindly to hooligans and street-fighting. Understand!"

David nodded and was lowered to the floor. His cool image had disappeared. Even his fringe hung limply across his forehead.

Caro rushed towards the dancers, searching for Michael. He was dancing with Aoife, whispering something into her ear. When she saw the expression on Caro's face she pulled away from him and came towards her.

"What are you crying for? What's up?"

"It's David. The bouncers. They've taken him outside." She had to shout above the music.

"What happened?" Michael was looking around in panic as if he had just noticed the disappearance of his right arm.

"They think he started a fight. But it was all Keith Fowler's fault."

By this stage Jennifer and Emma had stopped dancing.

With Michael hurrying in front of them, they went to the main entrance area of the community hall.

"Hey you!" Astonishment spread across the bouncer's face. "You were just barred from here. How the hell did you get back in?" He grabbed Michael by the front of his T-shirt and yanked him forward. "You're a cool boy, all right. First you sneak in without a membership card, then you start a fight and now you're back again after being barred. What kind of game do you think you're playing?"

"That was my twin brother you barred. Honest! I was dancing when it happened."

The bouncer looked towards his companion. "Hey, Loaf! This one's a laugh a minute. He's pulling the twin brother routine."

The other bouncer laughed and flapped his hand. "They all try that one." He stood like a black statue, solid and square in front of the exit. "I'll keep an eye on him while you go and ring the sergeant. He'll cool this fellow's heels for him."

"Faint," Jennifer hissed. "All of you, faint!"

With a loud groan she raised the back of her hand to her forehead and slumped to the floor. The bouncers watched, amazed when Aoife slumped beside her. Emma and Caro, knowing that the men would only believe so much, stayed where they were, making helpless sounds of alarm. The bouncer called Loaf ran towards them. Quick as a flash, Michael moved. By the time the girls had been revived and were obediently pushing their heads between their knees, he had disappeared through the exit.

"Were you girls drinking, taking anything?" demanded Loaf. He glanced suspiciously into Jennifer's eyes. Clear-eyed, she stared back at him. "It was the heat, Mister. I came out to get a breath of fresh air."

"It was my asthma," explained Aoife. She carried her asthma inhaler everywhere with her. The bouncer examined the pipe-like object, suspiciously. "I wouldn't put anything past you Beachwood Brats," he growled. "Where's that young punk gone?"

"I'll go and check the floor," said the second bouncer, walking towards the main hall.

"He left," said Caro. "I saw him running out when my friends fainted."

"Very convenient," growled the bouncer. "You'd better go back inside quick before I take a notion to bar the lot of you."

Instead of returning to the disco, they went to the mineral bar and bought bottles of Fanta.

"Well, that's got rid of my double troubles for the night." Jennifer tried to laugh but Caro could see that she was very upset. She was not the only one. Caro had been looking forward to having another dance with David. There was something nice about the way he made her feel. Her father told her that the memory of a first love stayed in one's mind forever. It was something precious. Not that she was in love with David Hilliard. She shook her head firmly. But maybe it was love. What did she know about love or life or sex or anything? Tonight would certainly stay in her mind for the rest of her life. She just hoped it would not blot out the nicer feeling. Suddenly she felt depressed. She hated those sudden mood swings. One minute she would be laughing at something stupid and then she would feel like bursting into tears for no reason that she could name.

"Growing pains," said her mother. This mysterious

condition covered everything from boredom, vague aches in her body, mood swings, to shadows under her eyes and tantrums.

"It's not fair," she sighed.

"What's not fair?" asked Aoife.

"Two dark heads," said Jennifer, trying to bang Caro and Aoife's heads together.

"Life's not fair," said Caro.

"Who on earth ever said it was?" said Emma, copying her mother's scolding voice. This made the girls giggle. But they still did not feel like dancing and settled down to wait until Jonathan arrived to bring them home.

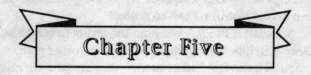

Chapter Five

At half-past eleven on the dot, Jonathan arrived. He had been to a concert at the Concert Hall and was humming snatches of *The Marriage of Figaro* when the girls clambered into the back seat. His car was spotless, an old Volkswagen Beetle that he had painted himself in a bright two-tone effect, yellow and brown. It was his pride and joy, with cutaway mudguards and flashy silver chrome. Anyone who rode in Jonathan's car had to obey certain rules. No smoking. No playing of any kind of pop music, rap, rock, hardcore, heavy metal, anything! No talking or giggling when he was listening to his tapes of classical music.

He worked in a financial institution and wore a cream trench coat that was too long for him. On cold days he knotted a belt casually around it but mostly it flapped open as he strode briskly down Grafton Street, swinging his briefcase. Caro had inspected his briefcase and discovered a half-eaten apple, an empty crisp packet, a copy of *Image Man* magazine and a book called *The Diary of Adrian Mole*. She believed that her eldest brother was pompous. Jennifer said that he was a yuppy. When he switched on his Nigel Kennedy tape, she tapped him on the shoulder. "Hey Jonathan. Don't play that rubbish. Put on some stuff we can all enjoy."

Sergeant Hilliard, having put the fear of God into his only daughter, had taught her to fear no other man.

Jonathan stared back at her through the driving mirror. His expression suggested that, in his bare feet, he had just stepped on a very slimy snail.

"In my car I am king," he said. "If you wish to walk home I can let you out right now. If you wish to stay in my kingdom, then I suggest you shut your mouth until I tell you otherwise."

Jennifer made a face but said nothing. Caro, in the front seat, knew that her friends were trying to stop giggling. She also knew that they would not succeed. But by the time their laughter escaped, Jonathan was carefully steering his car into the driveway. A dark shape flung itself on him, slobbering all over his tailored fawn slacks. Jonathan ignored this abuse and rubbed the auburn-coated setter's ears. "Hey, Rachmaninov. Take it easy. That's a good fellow."

At the front door, Rachmaninov (Jonathan had called him after his favourite composer) pushed past the girls and almost knocked them over in his efforts to get into the hall.

"Watch what you're doing, Rat Bag!" said Caro.

Jonathan stiffened. "How often do I have to tell you not to call my dog that ridiculous name? Even you, with your subnormal intellect, should be able to pronounce it properly."

"You're such a show-off," Caro huffed. "Why couldn't

you call your dog Spot or Rover or Puke-face. That's a good name. What's wrong with Puke-face?"

"Go to bed, little worm." Jonathan yawned. Rachmaninov followed him into the lounge and sprawled at his master's feet. The record player was turned on. Muted waves of classical music swept over the two of them. Jonathan sat back in his armchair, his face turned towards the ceiling, his hands conducting the orchestra. He refused all Caro's hints that he should take himself off to his bedroom.

"He's ruining my slumber party." She was furious with him. Earlier in the evening he had promised to go to bed as soon as he came in. The girls sat in the kitchen, waiting for the record to finish. When Caro looked into the lounge and saw him pouring out a glass of wine, she wanted to rush over and thump him on his chest. It was awful being the youngest in a family. She had no authority, whatsoever. Jonathan drank two glasses of wine before the record finished. Then he ordered Caro to make him tea and toast.

"There's brandy and duck paté in the fridge," he told her. "Spread it thinly on my toast and then cut the toast into triangles." He took his record off the turntable, carefully dusting it before putting it back in its sleeve. "Now, will I play another one before I go to bed?" he pondered.

"It's my slumber party," Caro shouted from the kitchen where she was scraping the burned surface off his toast. Jonathan pretended not to hear her. "Ah yes, Beethoven's Symphony Number 5. Would you like to hear that, Rachmaninov?"

"Woof! Woof!"

"Good fellow. I thought you would."

34

Music swelled once more.

"Pig! Pig! Pig!" stormed Caro. "He's doing that deliberately to wind me up." Jonathan had such a sick sense of humour. Suddenly she noticed a tin of dogfood. An idea flashed into her mind and was dismissed as being too awful for words. Almost immediately it returned, took root and stayed. Wide-eyed, the girls watched as Caro opened the tin and carefully, thinly, spread the dogfood over Jonathan's toast. Their faces grew red with suppressed laughter. Caro carried the toast into the lounge. Jennifer followed with the teapot. Aoife had his cup and saucer. Emma carried his teaspoon.

"Such attention," he said, as they hovered around him, pouring his tea, offering him toast and paté. They sat on the floor and watched as he raised the toast to his lips. He chewed slowly, deliberately, tapping his fingers to the strains of Beethoven.

Rachmaninov raised his elegant nose and sniffed.

"None for you, boy," said Jonathan. "You wouldn't appreciate it." He took a second bite and another. Jennifer was chewing her knuckles. Aoife had buried her face in her hands and was making snorting noises. Emma fled to the kitchen. Tears stood out on Caro's eyes and her insides ached and ached and ached from holding back her mirth.

"This is nice paté," said Jonathan. "They must have put some extra ingredient into it. Very meaty. A robust flavour." Jennifer, Aoife and Caro staggered to their feet and joined Emma in the kitchen.

"Do you girls ever do anything but giggle?" Jonathan shouted after them.

"I'll die. I'll die from laughing," gasped Jennifer. "Did you ever see anything like his face when he was trying to figure out that extra ingredient?"

"Goodnight girls! You can have the lounge now. I'm off to bed." His face froze when he noticed the open tin of dogfood on the kitchen counter and the smeared knife lying beside it. Caro grabbed it. "I was just going to feed Rat Bag," she said and offered a dainty triangle of dogfood paté on toast to the setter, who wolfed it down, delighted to be fed at such an unexpected hour.

"Don't give him bad habits," warned Jonathan, having dismissed his sudden sickening suspicion as too revolting even to consider. "Enjoy your slumber party, children, and don't stay up too late." He gave them a limp wave and went upstairs.

Over-the-top imagination, that was his problem. They wouldn't dare. He'd have noticed immediately. The desire to turn back and demand to know the truth made him pause on the stairs. But he could just imagine their horrible little faces and stifled giggles. On the landing, his stomach gave a heave and he burped loudly.

They could hear him pottering about. Jonathan took ages to go to bed. He was so methodical that he left his tie knotted and a strip of toothpaste on his brush in preparation for the following morning. Finally his bedroom door clicked closed. Thelma the cat mewed to come in for the night. Rachmaninov barked to go out. Silence fell. At last the girls had the house to themselves.

Chapter Six

I n the lounge, Caro switched on the lamp, over which she had draped a pale-pink scarf for special effect. She had bought joss sticks in the Stephen's Green Centre and their pungent scent caught against her breath when she lit them.

An hour later the girls had broken only one ground rule. But Mr Kane was still very annoyed when he came downstairs and interrupted Caro's demonstration of the modern dancing which she did every Saturday at The Dance Studio.

"Your father's a very grumpy man," said Emma, sounding quite subdued after he left.

"I know." Caro allowed herself to sulk for five minutes. He did not have to call her an "irritating little wart" in front of her friends. But she cheered up when she heard the sound of the pizza van. The girls ran to the door, afraid that a loud ring on the bell would wake Mr Kane again.

"Pepperoni, Hawaiian, à-la-jambon without tomato

and Pizza Palace Special without the olives," intoned a young man in a white jacket with "Patrick—the Pizza Prince" embroidered on the pocket.

Caro took the four large round cartons covered with garish illustrations and brought them inside. The Pizza Palace cartons always carried a picture on one side and a short story on the other side. It was a popular gimmick and the subject of each illustration began with the letter P. Caro had collected the Pizza Pig, Princess, Parrot, Pagoda and Panda. She was delighted to find that her carton contained the Pizza Poltergeist, a particularly horrifying image that glowed fearsomely in the dark when she turned off the lights.

"Sick!" said Aoife, who was trying to persuade Jennifer to swop her Pizza Princess for a Pizza Pig. The cartons made ideal bedroom posters, luminous discs glowing eerily from the walls. Inside the cartons, the contents were just as interesting and the girls sank their teeth into the cheesy toppings. Aoife glanced at the stacked bookshelves.

"What's that?" she asked, pointing to a white photo album.

"My parents' wedding album," replied Caro.

"Let's have a look," said Jennifer. The girls were always fascinated by photo albums, provided that they were of someone else's family. The sight of Mr Kane with sideburns and a top hat made them laugh. But the sight of all the female guests in mini-dresses reduced them to a respectful silence.

"I didn't know they wore minis in the olden days," said Aoife.

"They must have," said Caro, staring at her Aunt Anita, who had become as plump and sleek as a seal. But on that special day, she looked as thin as a stick in a mini-dress that hung around her bottom like a fringe.

"Isn't that Beachwood Strand?" asked Emma, pointing to a windblown shot of Mrs Kane, clutching her wedding veil, with a background of waves.

"Yeah! They were married in the Swansbury Hotel," said Caro. The Swansbury Hotel was the local hotel. "In fact," she lowered her voice and pointed to the photograph. "It was on that spot that my dad proposed to my mother."

"Never!" chorused the girls. "Tell us!"

This story always reduced the Kane family to howls of disbelief whenever either of their parents could be persuaded to repeat it. Twenty-two years previously, on a sunny day in July, Kevin Kane wrote *Stella McNulty, I love you, Please marry me* on the wet sands of Beachwood Strand. He and Stella were due to meet at half-past three that afternoon. But he had forgotten that tide and time waits for no woman and Stella McNulty was always late. On this occasion, she had discovered a puncture on the front wheel of her bicycle and, unaware that her boyfriend had just penned the most important question of his life, was in the kitchen of her house repairing it.

When she wheeled her bike along the strand an hour and a half later, her boyfriend was ankle-deep in sandy swirling water. The tide was coming in, fast. She wondered at his furious face, and why his elephant flares were soaking wet to his knees. Mostly she wondered why he was helplessly trying to keep the tide at bay. Of his message there was no sign.

"It was written in the sands of time and, like my love for you, it has been swept away forever," he shouted at her.

At this stage of the story the friends laughed so loudly that Caro had to hush them up. But she was giggling just as much at the thought of her father speaking like that— and wearing elephant flares!

It was only when a wave soaked the ankles of Stella McNulty (soon to be Kane), and then surged backwards like a conjuror revealing secrets, that she saw the wavering, almost washed-away line of letters. She had no difficulty recognising the question. Bending down she wrote *Yes, Yes, Yes, Yes* all along the wet sand until Kevin Kane toppled her into the soapy waves and covered her face with kisses.

"Just as well the tide rolled back or you wouldn't be here," said Aoife in a thoughtful voice.

"That's gross," declared Caro, shuddering. To owe your existence to something as fragile as a passing wave was a humbling thought.

With such happy memories of Beachwood, it was not surprising that Caro's parents decided to settle in the area after their marriage. By that time, the grounds and stately home of the Hobourne family had been sold and Oaktree Estate was in the process of being built. Soon after they moved into their new house Jonathan was born. Two years later Susan came along and, after another two-year gap, it was Danny's turn. Following the same time span, Caro was born, and always felt rather peeved that the next bi-annual addition to her family had been a dishwasher. Even though it was very handy, it didn't compare with a younger sister. She put the photo album back on the shelf and the four girls, chewing the last slices of pizza, settled down to watch *Child's Play 2*. It was so scary that no one was aware of the tapping noise on the window. But when the soundtrack died for a moment they heard it.

"What's that?" demanded Caro. She lowered the video. The others listened. Silence. They started chewing again. Tap, tap, tap on the window pane.

"It's a branch from the sycamore tree," guessed Aoife, wiping melted cheese from her chin. She pulled across the curtains and glanced out the window. The branch of the tree was motionless in the calm night air.

"It's our imagination," she decided.

Scratch, scratch, scratch on the window pane.

"It's the cat trying to get in," guessed Emma.

"I've just fed an anchovy to the cat," whispered Jennifer. "She's under the table."

They stared at each other, beginning to shiver as a low voice began to speak.

"Caro…Caro…Caro. I'm coming to get you. Hee Hee Ha Ha Hee Hee Ha Ha!" The sound was barely audible, as if the words flattened themselves against the glass and tried to break into the comfortable lounge where the four girls sat, stiff-backed with terror.

"You look out this time and see who it is, Caro," suggested Emma. She buried her face in a cushion.

"Why should I be the one?" hissed Caro.

"It's your house," replied Emma, her face burrowing deeper when the strange weird giggle grew louder.

"Could it be Patrick the Pizza Prince trying to freak us?" whispered Aoife.

"Caro…Caro. I am the ghost of Cross Hollow. I'm lonely and cold. The clay is heavy on my heart. Let me in…please Caro…let me in."

Emma started to sob. The pizza base in Caro's mouth turned to rubber and goosebumps chased each other up and down her arms.

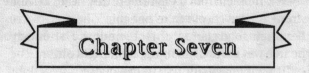

Chapter Seven

They knew all about the ghost of Cross Hollow. This headless male figure was reputed to be Lord Norton Hobourne, who had died in 1769. Since then, his ghost was supposed to haunt Cross Hollow, a sweeping valley of land that used to be part of the Hobourne Estate. Rows of trees divided it into the shape of a cross and one section of it had become the Cross Hollow Garden Centre. It was rumoured that the ghost could still be seen in the shadow of the trees, stumbling blindly while he searched for his head. There were also stories of ghostly sightings of his head in the nearby woodlands, Twist and Shake, where this gruesome object was supposed to be hidden.

The woodlands had been nicknamed Twist and Shake because they were such an eerie wilderness of rotten tree stumps and tangled undergrowth. If Caro and her friends ventured too far into the woodlands, they trembled and clutched each other when creepers and trailing branches brushed against their faces.

"Shush a minute," ordered Jennifer. She cupped her

hand around her ear. The thought that it could be an earthly voice made the girls listen more carefully.

"Caro, I am crying. Sobbing in the lost night. I want to find my head but the clay is heavy on my heart. Release me from my grave...please release me!"

Jennifer interrupted this lament by shouting something quite vile and unrepeatable. Once more, she pulled back the curtains. Two shapes ducked out of sight underneath the window-ledge.

"It's Michael and David!" Jennifer was furious. "They must have sneaked out. Mam sleeps like a log and wouldn't hear a bomb exploding under her bed. OK, Double Trouble. You're dead!" Even as she spoke she was running out to the hall and opening the front door. From behind her, Caro could see the twins as they dashed out of the front gate.

"Come on, girls. Let's catch them," Jennifer growled.

"Let them go. Come back," wailed Caro. "I promised not to leave the house."

But Aoife and Emma, caught up in the excitement of the chase, had followed Jennifer and were racing up Oaktree Avenue. With a deep sigh of resignation, Caro quietly closed the front door and set off in pursuit.

Emma was fast, a champion sprinter in the Community Games. But on Oaktree Green, a shrubbery and play area, she tripped over a piece of wood. Jennifer passed her out, long legs pumping, gaining on Michael. She jumped on his back and clung fast. The two of them fell on the grass.

"Smart guy," snarled Jennifer, locking his arm behind his back. "I'm going to make you pay."

"It was just a joke. Where's your sense of humour?" Michael tried to fend her off. "Ouch! That hurts. Don't be such a bitch."

David, realising that his twin had fallen, returned to rescue him in the same instant that Aoife, Emma and Caro arrived. They were breathless and exhilarated from running through the shrubbery on Oaktree Green at such a late hour. The street lights and a clear moon made their faces shadowy and gaunt.

David circled the girls, trying to look intimidating. Jennifer cast a scornful glare at him then returned her attention to Michael. "What will we do with him, girls? Shall we feed him grass or whip him with pine needle branches or dance on his fingers. You choose, Caro. It's your party he spoiled."

"I don't think I want to do anything so extreme," replied Caro, wondering if living with five boys was good for the gentler side of Jennifer's personality. She also wondered how, with a father as strict as the sergeant, the Hilliards were the wildest family on Oaktree Estate. "Why don't you just let him go. He's suffered enough."

"Huh! She doesn't bother me. I'm only humouring her…ouch…ow!"

All further sounds were absorbed in the grass as Jennifer shoved Michael's face into the earth, then jumped up. "That's the end of your running career, for sure. You'll never be able to catch me now," she hissed, begging to be chased.

"Shush!" Caro was cringing, terrified that the neighbours would hear them. But when David began lumbering towards her, imitating a gorilla, she joined the three girls and sped through Oaktree Green, dodging in and out of the shrubbery, knowing that the boys were only an arm's length away. The loop from the waistband of her jeans snagged in a branch and she impatiently pulled herself free. At last, exhausted, they collapsed on the ground. There was space between the bushes which shielded them from view and the branches formed a roof over their heads. When they were younger, the girls had often made it their den. The boys slumped beside them. The breath whistled in their lungs.

"Go on. Admit you were scared," David ordered the girls.

"You must be joking," snorted Jennifer. "I'd be more scared of a butterfly."

"Liar," chorused the twins.

"I bet you believe all that garbage about the ghost of Cross Hollow," said David.

"That's because it's true," said Aoife.

"Rubbish!"

"It *is* true," repeated Aoife. "I know the full story. I read it in a history book." She settled her bottom into a more comfortable position and lowered her voice. All thoughts of returning to Caro's house were forgotten. There was something strange and exciting about the night smells and the shadows that surrounded them.

"Tell us about it then," said David, trying to slide his arm around Caro's shoulder.

"We don't want to know. Please don't tell us," begged Caro, giving a shivery laugh and pushing David's arm away. She knew what Aoife's vivid imagination could do to her nerves.

"Go on. Tell us," ordered Michael, enjoying the sight of the three girls drawing closer to each other. Each time Aoife told this story it was different. Her friends were no sooner used to one horror scene than she changed it to something more gruesome. Her long curly hair was caught up in a ponytail but even though it was dragged back from her high forehead, the curls escaped in a frizzy halo around her face. She had a dreamy look in her eyes which meant that her imagination was in full flow. With a sigh of contentment they settled down to listen to the latest version of the story of the ghost of Cross Hollow.

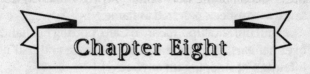

Chapter Eight

"It happened on a dark winter's night many hundreds of years ago. 1769 to be exact, the night that Hobourne Castle burned to the ground. A wild night of storms and high winds that howled over the sea, and dashed against the walls of Hobourne Castle. At the back of the castle, there were small cottages, homes for the families who laboured on the estate for Lord Norton Hobourne, the most cruel Hobourne of all time. Within the cottages, children huddled, shivering. They could hear it, deep in the throat of the wind; the sound of a banshee keening.

"'Listen to the banshee cry,' they said to their parents. 'She is crying because Lord Norton Hobourne is forcing a child-bride to marry him.'

"'Go to sleep now and do not let your imagination play such foolish tricks,' ordered their parents.

"'But it's true. It's true! Look at how the night burns. It is telling us that in the dawning hours, Lord Norton Hobourne will burn the youth from his child-bride.'

"'What nonsense is this?' scolded their parents and, blowing out the candles, left their children in the dark. The children ran to the windows. High about the trees, the endless valleys and hills of swaying branches, they saw the banshee's hair, red as flame."

"Shut up! Shut up!" moaned Caro, putting her hands over her ears. But Aoife had an audience and had no intention of stopping for anyone.

"I'll catch you if you faint," David murmured.

"Thanks for nothing," Caro replied, pretending not to notice his arm when it slipped around her waist.

"The banshee keened as she combed her hair. Her fiery tresses spread across the sky until the night was as bright as day and it seemed as if the flames of hell had escaped. But no adult saw this strange sight and in Hobourne Castle, Lord Norton Hobourne prepared for his wedding. It was said that he had married many times in secret and murdered each wife as soon as he grew tired of her. Their bodies were taken out at dead of night and buried in Cross Hollow.

"He intended marrying a beautiful young girl who was just fourteen. Anna Mangan was her name, and she was the daughter of a man who worked in the piggery on Hobourne Estate. Lord Hobourne had ordered him to bring his daughter to Hobourne Castle so that the wedding could take place at dawn. The arranged wedding was a dark secret. If Anna's father mentioned one word to anyone, Lord Hobourne had threatened to throw the Mangan family off their land. The father was overwhelmed at the idea of his daughter marrying a lord. What riches. What fame for their family. Surely, once the wedding had taken place, Lord Hobourne would have to introduce his Lady Anna to the world.

"Anna Mangan had pleaded with her father to refuse Lord Hobourne's offer. She had wept and covered his hand with kisses. It was no use. Her father had worked too long in the piggery and had both the greed and the manners of the swine he tended. In other words, he was a sexist pig!"

"Stop scoring points and continue," ordered Michael. The twins' expressions were rapt with interest.

"Her friends wondered at Anna's grief, at her pale face, at the deep shadows beneath her eyes. She told them what Lord Hobourne planned but swore them to secrecy. Sadly, they had watched her as she walked towards the castle. They bid her a silent goodbye when the heavy oak doors clanged behind her. That night, when they listened to the banshee keen, they heard a story. The story of all the young girls who had entered the castle and had never again seen the light of day."

Aoife sighed, lost in thought, then discreetly checked the luminous hand of her wristwatch. It told both time and date.

"Lord Hobourne intended that his wedding would take place at dawn on the twenty-fourth day of August," she continued.

"That's today," squeaked Emma.

"Yes, it is." Aoife's voice deepened. "This is the anniversary of that hideous ceremony."

"'Come with me. Come with me. Come with me,' keened the banshee when the night had turned to dawn. They left their beds, all the children of Hobourne Estate, and followed the sound of that keening wail. The fiery sky lit their way. The wind blew behind them and it seemed as if they floated through air until they reached a valley. It was covered in mist but when they began to descend into it, the wind blew the mist away and they saw humps of earth in the shape of graves. On each grave small white stones shone. They spelled out a bitter epitaph. *Here lies a wife of Norton Hobourne. His property.*

"'Remove the stones. Remove the stones. Remove the stones,' commanded the keening voice. Each child bent down and lifted some stones, small pebbles, as cold as ice. Their hands became numb and the chill spread through them so that they were unable to move. But the light from the fiery tresses of the banshee fell across them and the heat began to return to their bodies.

"In Hobourne Castle, Lord Norton Hobourne took the young girl, Anna Mangan, by the hand and led her to the altar. There was no minister of God present to perform the ceremony, only a minister of the devil, an evil-looking man with the nose of a pig and black teeth. He was the only adult who could hear the keen of the banshee. The fury of the sound frightened him, especially when he heard the banshee ordering the children to remove the white stones. He had buried Lord Hobourne's wives and placed the stones on their graves to keep their restless spirits imprisoned. If the children removed the stones the spirits would escape and destroy his lord and master.

"'Noble Lord, we must postpone the marriage ceremony," he cried. "The banshee plans mischief on the wild wind of dawn.'

"'You are a superstitious fool," roared Lord Hobourne. "Make this child my wife. I am eager for the delights of young flesh.'

"So the evil minister began the marriage ceremony. But when it was Anna Mangan's turn to say 'I do,' she hesitated. The thought of her parents and her younger brothers and sisters having to leave their home had made her accept the fact that she must marry Lord Hobourne. But she also heard the banshee keen, "Your marriage vow is your death vow." This warning was repeated three times.

"'You can force me to the altar steps, my Lord," she cried. 'You can force me into your bed. You can imprison me forever. But you cannot make me say those words.'

"'Then I will cut out your tongue and feed it to my dogs,' roared Lord Hobourne.

"'Noooooooooooooooooo!' cried the wind.

"'Neverrrrrrrrrrrrrr!' keened the banshee.

"'Freedommmmmmmmmmmm!' screamed the ghostly wives of Lord Hobourne.

"The words 'I do' were never uttered. Instead the wind blew through the castle, blew out the candles and the devil's prayer book from the minister's hands. For the first, and last, time Lord Norton Hobourne heard the banshee keen. But the other sound, the sound that filled him with terror, was the cry of freedom and revenge that came from the throats of his murdered wives as they arose from their graves in the grey misty dawn light. They entered the castle, an army of white spectres, and, with joyous shrieks, tore their husband apart, limb from limb. Before he could blink his eyes, he was beheaded. They flung his head out the window and it did not rest until it reached the deepest, darkest part of Twist and Shake. Before he could lift an arm it dangled from the ceiling. What a time they had. A massacre. And they howled the whole way through it. Then they..."

"That's enough," moaned Caro, giving David an excuse to tighten his arm around her. Even he was looking ill. "That's the most disgusting, gross, revolting story you have ever told. And every word of it's a lie."

"No, it's not." Aoife stood up, annoyed that her literary talents should be so insulted. "Every word of it's true. Lord Norton Hobourne is the ghost of Cross Hollow. The headless ghost. The banshee's hair set fire to the castle and that was why it burned to the ground."

"What happened to Anna Mangan?" asked Emma. Her eyes shone, deep green pools of fear.

"Let me see..." Aoife thought for a moment. "The children broke open the oak door and carried her back to her family. The next day they placed the white stones back on the graves. But this time they arranged them in the shape of a cross and that was why the valley became known as Cross Hollow."

"You're the world's best liar," said Jennifer. Aoife's imagination always filled her with admiration.

"You can laugh all you like," said Aoife, beginning to walk back towards Caro's house. "But we'll see which side of your face you're laughing from when you see the ghost of Cross Hollow's head grinning down at you from the trees. And don't say I didn't warn you!"

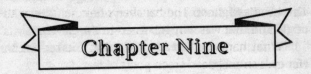

Chapter Nine

"Aren't you going to bring us in? You can't expect us to walk home alone after telling us a story like that." Michael sounded outraged. "We could be attacked by a banshee."

"Tough luck," said Jennifer.

"Just bring us in for a slice of pizza," David leaned over the gate and grasped Caro's hand. "We're starving. There's no food in the fridge. Only dry cheese and even the mouse won't eat that. Honest!"

"Watch my heart bleed," said Caro, trying to pull her hand away. "What would your father say if he could see you now?"

"He's on night duty. He's too busy cleaning up The Slopes to worry about us."

"You'll be in big trouble if Ma catches you," warned his sister.

David shrugged. "She took some tablets for her headache and that always makes her sleep like a log."

Mrs Hilliard was famous for her headaches. She claimed

they were brought on by living with five noisy sons and a daughter who was louder than the whole lot of them put together. Not to mention "the sergeant" (Caro had never heard her call her husband anything else) and the way he barked commands at everyone, including the budgie. And even the budgie never shut up singing. Mrs Hilliard regularly took headache tablets and no one in Oaktree blamed her.

Caro was growing nervous again. If her parents woke up and heard the boys' voices it would be goodbye to slumber parties for the rest of her life. Eventually the twins accepted that pizza sharing and mixed slumber parties were not on. They headed towards Oaktree Drive, shoulders slouched, toes dragging the ground in mock-disappointment. Caro felt the belt loop of her jeans where her key-ring normally hung. Instead of the cold feel of metal, she touched the frayed edges of a torn loop.

"Oh no! My keys." Frantically her fingers touched the other loops, remembering in dismay how her jeans had snagged on a branch during the chase. "What'll we do? Mam will have a stroke if I ring the doorbell and she finds out we've been running around the green."

"We'd better go back and look for them," suggested Aoife. They returned to the green, crawling around on all fours. Jennifer gave a furious "Ruff Ruff" and tried to bite Caro on her neck.

"Lay off, you pitbull!" begged Caro. She knew she should not feel like laughing. "This is serious!" But she could not resist giving a high-pitched yelp and trying to bite Jennifer's chin. They crawled through thick shrubbery, ran their hands over the grass, pleaded with the keys to reveal themselves. No luck.

"Do you know something, girls?" declared Emma.

"We're in deep trouble."

Caro was growing desperate. With Aoife and Jennifer, she knelt down on the green and said an Act of Sorrow. It was recited with great fervour. To be on the safe side, Emma, who was Church of Ireland, then said an Our Father in an effort to waken the Lord. But he (or *she*, said Aoife who felt that such issues needed airing) was not in a listening mood and, eventually, grass-stained and weary, the girls admitted defeat.

"What about the bathroom? Is the top window ever left open?" asked Jennifer. She regularly escaped from her house by this route when she was supposed to be studying. But that was because her father had built an extension to their kitchen and the roof was just a short drop beneath her. Caro shook her head. There was no handy roof to climb over and, even if there was, Mr Kane was careful to check the lock on every window at night.

"We could throw stones at Jonathan's window?" suggested Emma.

"No way. Even an earthquake wouldn't waken him once he goes to sleep. Danny's as bad. And Susan's down at the beach party."

"The beach party!" Jennifer's eyes gleamed with excitement. "That's it. Susan will have a key. We can go down to the beach and find the party."

Caro considered this idea. It spelled serious trouble. Oaktree Green was bad enough. But if her parents heard she was running around a beach at night...Her mind could not go beyond that point.

"Well, what do you think?" demanded Jennifer. "We can hide out here all night and bore the pants off each other. Or do something really exciting like going to the beach and getting a key."

"We might be seen going through the village. There are bound to be people down there still. Supposing they tell our parents," worried Caro.

"We could go through Hobourne Park," suggested Aoife.

"Oh no. I couldn't!" Emma shivered. "Not after that sick story you told us."

"Don't be such cowards. You know there wasn't a word of truth in what she told us." Jennifer looked scornfully at Aoife, who stared right back with her "you'll see" expression. "We've had enough nonsense about the ghost of Cross Hollow for one night." She stood before them, hands on hips, the picture of determination. "It'll only take a few minutes if we go through Hobourne. Come on."

She began to stride across Oaktree Green.

"Wait for us," said Emma, sprinting after her.

The three girls flitted between clumps of bushes. Occasional lights shone from upstairs windows but otherwise the houses were in darkness. They moved cautiously towards Oaktree Drive, the last row of houses on their estate. Behind the houses a high wall formed the boundaries of Hobourne Park. There were jutting stones at various points in the brickwork and, over the years, these had provided hand and footholds for those who climbed it. Mainly it provided a much-used shortcut for the Beachwood Comprehensive pupils who lived nearby.

"It's just as well to get some practice in again," said Aoife, as she scaled the wall. "From next week we'll be doing this every day."

This realisation brought a muted groan from everyone. The stately house had lost some, but not all, of its stateliness when it became the local comprehensive school and whenever first year pupils entered through the wooden double-doors into the chilly, high-ceilinged hall, they always automatically lowered their voices, as if sensing the disapproval of the Hobourne ancestors. But the girls were starting second year and the glamour of being secondary school pupils had worn off.

The drop from the wall into Hobourne Park was steep. They jumped lightly down, walking close together along the narrow path. It was a balmy night. A warm breeze passed over the trees without rustling the leaves. It was the first time the girls had ever seen Hobourne Park in darkness. Familiar sights looked different. Moonlight played with their fears, splashing long, skinny shadows before them. The girls passed a row of stables that had been turned into Beachwood Youth Club and the Hobourne Athletics Centre, where Emma's star shone bright.

Occasionally scare stories about Hobourne Park did the rounds of Beachwood. Sometimes young people were warned not to use the public section of the park because a suspicious stranger had tried to talk to children. There were stories about lager parties and drugs being sold to anyone with money to buy. No one knew if these stories were true but they added to their fears as they walked along. To their relief, the park appeared to be deserted. They were walking through a piece of history to which, until 1970, no one except the Hobourne family had access.

A night dew lay on the grass as they passed the Gaelic and soccer pitches.

"I'm exhausted. Are we ever going to reach the strand?" moaned Emma.

They had forgotten how long it took to walk through

Hobourne Park. In the children's playground they pushed each other on the swings and tried out the see-saw.

The ruins of the old castle looked grim and mysterious in the moonlight. Weeds pushed through the brickwork and a tall, slanting tree grew out of an old fireplace. The castle fire had not been caused, as Aoife claimed, by the rising of Lord Hobourne's dead wives. Lord Hobourne was a drunk, a gambler, a nasty piece of goods who raged through his castle one night and set fire to a row of priceless tapestries in the Long Hall. The flames quickly spread and he died in the blaze. It was said that his screams woke the entire population of Beachwood and that the castle glowed in a red flame for two days afterwards. As every servant and member of the Hobourne family escaped except Lord Hobourne, it was suspected that he had been murdered before he had a chance to flee. Some people believed that it was his eldest son who committed the deed while the fire raged and that he had buried his father's body in Cross Hollow in case any evidence would be discovered among the charred remains. A more popular version had been passed down by one of Lord Hobourne's servants, who claimed that an ornamental sword hanging above the castle door fell and cut off Lord Hobourne's head. The head rose in the air with an almighty roar and was last seen above the trees of Twist and Shake. But everyone agreed that Aoife's story about the dead wives was a far more interesting version.

Many people claimed to know someone who had seen the headless Lord Hobourne. He left his grave at night to return to his castle where he knelt in prayer until dawn, begging his head to reveal its whereabouts. Caro could not understand how he could say prayers if he had no head. But Emma said he prayed from his heart. If someone was brave enough to run backwards around the castle on the stroke of midnight, they would be able to see him.

It was now past midnight, half-past two, to be exact, but nevertheless, the girls looked in the opposite direction as they passed the ruins. When they heard a voice, a clipped voice that sounded noble and ghostly, they stopped dead.

"Is he saying prayers?" Caro's heart pounded.

No one had the courage to reply.

"This is the spot where the sword hung," said the voice. "So if there is any truth to that particular story, the beheading would have taken place in this vicinity."

"The second story is more believable," a female voice answered. "If he was beheaded by his son it could also have been at this point. Perhaps the old servant saw what happened but out of loyalty to the new Lord Hobourne, invented the story of the sword."

"Mrs Boggan," breathed Caro, limp with relief.

"That must be Professor Price," said Aoife. "I'd love to meet him."

"Don't be mad." Jennifer wiped her forehead. "If they saw us they would insist on bringing us home. I want to go to the beach party."

"I thought we were going there to collect the key." Caro was suspicious of Jennifer's enthusiasm. "We're going home immediately afterwards."

"Of course we are," replied Jennifer.

"Is there any evidence that anyone ever dug up Cross Hollow to see if Lord Hobourne's remains were buried there?" asked the professor.

"There's no record of that ever happening," replied

Mrs Boggan. "Mainly it's just local legend, and there are so many different stories of how his death occurred that it's hard to untangle the truth."

"We have plenty of time, sweet Miranda," said the professor. He chuckled. "I rather think I'm going to enjoy my research on this book."

A short silence followed.

"Really, Professor Price. What if the ghost of Cross Hollow is watching you?" Mrs Boggan sounded very amused.

"Then all he can do is envy me," replied the professor. The girls fled.

"Do you think he was getting off? You know...deep kissing with...sweet Miranda?" Jennifer choked on the name. She was beginning to see Mrs Boggan in a new light.

"Don't be so disgusting," said Caro. "He sounded ancient. Do you ever manage to think about anything but sex, Jennifer Hilliard?"

"With great difficulty," retorted Jennifer, wild and unruly daughter of Sergeant Hilliard.

They climbed a gate leading from the park and darted across the road. Within a few minutes they were on Beachwood Strand. The moon was bright, clear and full, lighting their way. They ran towards the top of the sand dunes. With a shriek of delight Caro flung herself over the edge, jumping, with the ease of long practice, into the soft sand below. The others followed, returning again and again to the summit of the dunes. It was exhilarating. Sometimes, instead of jumping, they slid down the dunes on their stomachs, or allowed their bodies to roll over and over, sand spraying around them, gritty on their lips, tickling their toes.

"I've never had so much fun in all my life," declared Emma. "This is the best slumber party ever!"

"We'd better find the beach party before we're discovered," said Caro. Despite the excitement and the fun, a knot of fear had tightened her chest at the thought of meeting Susan. Supposing she told her mother or, worse still, supposing her mother or father woke up? The party was being held further down the beach at a spot called The Slopes where the dunes curved into grassy heights and hollows, an ideal sheltered place for a bonfire. Narrow flattened paths were hidden between high clumps of grass. A private place to park cars if you were young and in love. This was one place where Sergeant Hilliard waged his morality campaign.

"Do you know what they do in The Slopes when the passion killers arrive?" Aoife asked. "The couple parked in the first car blast the horn when they see the torch. They have a special signal. When the next car hears the signal the driver blasts the horn on that car and so on until all the cars parked on the Strand know that the passion killers are on their rounds and take off."

"Weird," said Caro. The idea that a day would ever come when they would want to park in a car with a boy seemed quite unbelievable. But that did not stop them being interested in the carry-on of those older brothers and sisters who did. Faintly they heard the sound of singing from The Slopes.

"That's it," said Aoife. "Let's go."

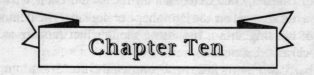

Chapter Ten

E ven with a full moon it was difficult to see. The girls staggered when their feet stepped into hidden sand hollows, felt their clothes catching in scraggy clumps of gorse. The singing grew louder.

"I have fallen for another. She can make her own way home." Jennifer sang along with the unseen voice, imitating the Saw Doctors. "I bet that's Greg Power singing. He sang that song in your house at your Christmas party, Aoife."

Aoife nodded and shushed her up. When they climbed the springy grass and looked down into a hollow, they saw a circle of older teenagers and young people in their early twenties, swaying together and singing along with him. A bonfire blazed, shooting sparks into the darkness. Guitars were being played by a woman and man. Beer cans lay scattered around the fire. There was no sign of Susan. Nor could they see her friend, Andrea Stone, in whose house Susan intended spending the night.

Greg stopped singing. He opened a can of beer.

"That's thirsty work," he yelled above the clapping. He drank deeply and smacked his lips.

"There's Paul," whispered Caro.

Aoife's brother sat beside a girl with short hair, cut in a bob that set off the elfin shape of her face. The flames lit her slanting eyes, her kittenish smile when she snuggled closely against him.

"Sonia Hanson's a cow," muttered Caro. "She's doing that deliberately because Susan fancies him." She could never understand why Susan had become friendly with Sonia Hanson during her final year in Beachwood Comprehensive. As far as Caro could see, they had nothing in common except an interest in Paul Johnston.

"Did you see that?" hissed Aoife. Paul had buried his face in Sonia's neck.

"I think he's nibbling her ear," said Jennifer in a know-it-all voice.

"Gross," said Emma. "Poor Susan. Do you think that's why she's not here? Maybe she couldn't stand watching them and went back to Andrea's house."

"Don't say that," whimpered Caro, already suspecting that this was true. "We've *got* to get that key. She *has* to be around somewhere."

"Maybe she's gone for a walk in the dunes with someone..." Jennifer glanced meaningfully at Caro.

"Don't be so disgusting. My sister's not like that." Caro stared in disgust at Paul and Sonia.

While the others continued to sing, the young couple slipped away towards Mr Johnston's car. It was parked on a grassy space surrounded by high dunes, out of sight of the beach party. The lights flashed on for an instant when the door opened.

"I hope the passion killers get them!" Emma glared at

the dark and private car. Caro's friends liked Susan. She lent them books and records, always remembered their birthdays and was willing to answer in a straightforward way any questions about sex and love and being a teenager.

"Why don't we get them!" There was a thoughtful note in Jennifer's voice. She began to move towards the parked car. The windows were steamy and it was impossible to see through them.

"We can't." Caro was shocked. "Supposing they are…you know…"

"Well, they shouldn't be," Jennifer reasoned. "We have to help my father in his morality campaign."

"That's true," said Aoife, who was curious to see why the windows were so steamed up. Knowing what was happening beyond them would give her tremendous power over her elder brother. "We're doing this for Susan."

"Shhhh! Stop laughing. They'll hear us," warned Caro.

Two girls went to one side of the car. The others crawled around to the far side. At a signal from Jennifer, they jumped together, yelling, pressing their faces and hands against the glass.

"The passion killers are here," shrieked Jennifer.

The couple in the back seat sprang apart, dazed faces turning towards the flattened noses and puckered lips at the window. A female scream rang out. Then another. It was soon drowned in a shrill blast as Paul reached for the horn.

"Run!" shrieked Jennifer. "Run for your life!"

The girls ran through the high grass and flung themselves behind a bush. Another car horn took up the signal. Soon The Slopes rang with the sound of car horns. Headlights sprayed light over the dunes. Engines revved and cars suddenly appeared, all heading out of Beachwood Strand.

"What have we done?" said Jennifer, awed by all the activity.

"Did you see his face?" gasped Emma.

"I'm never going to let a boy do anything like that to me," declared Caro, on a shivery breath of excitement.

"They were only kissing," said Jennifer, disappointed. "I'd hoped to see some real action."

Caro wondered if she would ever be able to look at Paul Johnston again without blushing. Probably not. She also figured that Susan's chances of going to the debs with him were pretty slim.

The people at the beach party had jumped to their feet when the horns started blasting and were laughing and hollering after the cars. When the last car disappeared and there seemed to be no sign of the passion killers, they settled back around the fire.

"Hey Susan! Give us some Mary Coughlan," shouted Greg Power.

"Susan's gone. She went ages ago," a female voice replied.

"I didn't see her going." Greg sounded surprised. "Damn. I love the way she does "'Delaney's Gone Back on the Wine.'"

"Then you'd better go back on the beer. 'Cause she ain't here," the voice retorted. "She went off with Andrea."

Gradually the singing resumed.

"So now, Bright Spark! What's your next brilliant idea?" Caro asked.

Jennifer was unrepentant. "It's not my fault that

Susan went off in a huff because of Paul Johnston. Someone else can think of an idea for a change."

"Caro, who's the first member of your family to get up in the morning?" asked Emma.

"Danny. He goes jogging at some unearthly hour. I think it's around six. He says it's the only time he can be sure that the air's not polluted."

"He must be nuts," said Jennifer.

"Environmentally nutty," laughed Emma. She checked her watch. "It's now three o'clock. That's only a few hours away. We'll catch Danny when he's leaving and slip back in. How's that?"

"What do we do until then?" moaned Aoife. "I'm exhausted."

"Let's get away from here in case we're seen," suggested Caro.

They stole away, silent shapes flitting between the dunes. Soon they could no longer hear the music. Apart from a lone seagull that cawked angrily at them, there was no other sign of life on the beach. They tried to figure out where exactly Mr Kane had written his passionate proposal.

"It could have been anywhere," declared Emma, looking at the calm sea. When the tide was out, everyone moaned about the "miles and miles" of squiggly sand they had to walk over before they could even wet their toes. Tonight, the tide was full in, gentle rolling waves lapping the sand. The girls stopped walking when they reached Shale Head, a high rock formation in the shape of a half moon. Slippery with seaweed and slime, it loomed above them.

"I know something that will keep us awake." The thoughtful note in Jennifer's voice filled Caro with dread. "Let's go for a moonlight swim in Shale Cove."

"Oh no," moaned Caro. "That's the worst idea I ever heard."

"It's not. It's brilliant," said Jennifer. "Just think! It's a lovely night. The water will be like soup."

Shale Cove lay between the curving half-moon shape of the Head and was a popular place for mothers with young children. Even at full tide the water was shallow enough for safe swimming. Jennifer was winding them up with her enthusiasm. "It's fantastic. Just imagine...we can tell our grandchildren that we swam on Beachwood Strand in the small hours of the morning."

"But we won't have any grandchildren if we drown," wailed Caro.

"No one ever drowns in Shale Cove," argued Jennifer. "But, if it makes you happy, we'll swim parallel to shore."

"We don't have any bathing suits." Caro knew she was fighting a losing battle.

"Yes, we have," insisted Jennifer. "We have our birthday suits."

This suggestion was so daring that it silenced everyone for a few minutes.

"You mean skinny-dipping," gasped Emma folding her hands protectively across her chest.

"In the nude!" whispered Aoife. "I couldn't. That's embarrassing."

Jennifer began to dance around them. "Come on...come on...come on. Skinny-dipping by moonlight. What a slumber party!"

She pulled her sweatshirt over her head and ran towards the opening between the rocks that led into Shale Cove. "I'm going for a swim and if no one else wants to come with me, I'm going on my own." Just before she reached the water she took off her bra and panties and flung them over the nearest rock. Her bottom gleamed white in the darkness for an instant before she dipped her body under the water.

"She's awful," gasped Aoife. "I'm not taking off my clothes."

"It's fantastic!" Jennifer's voice boomed back at them. "Brilliant! Come on."

Emma began to undress. "Let's wear our bra and panties. We can pretend they're a bikini."

This seemed like an ideal compromise. Quick as a flash, before they could change their minds, the three girls undressed.

"Here we go...here we go...here we go..." chanted Emma, leading the way.

A sudden chorus of screams echoed along the beach. They dipped and surfaced, hands flailing, water splashing. Waves washed over them, leaving them breathless with shock and excitement. They held hands and formed a circle, ducking down at Jennifer's command. Then Caro was free from her friends, floating in a pool of silver, stars piercing the darkness, more and more stars appearing until the sky was no longer black but streaked with a milky banner of light. Like the vast, mysterious universe, her slumber party was spinning out of control. Never in all her life had she been so disobedient. Never in all her life had she felt so wonderful. Tomorrow and the consequences belonged to another time dimension.

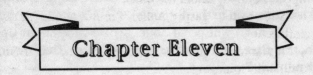

Chapter Eleven

O nce they were out of the water the girls jogged along the sand, their bodies tingling from the sea. "Whoo...ahhh! Whoo...ahhh! Whooo....ahhh!" warbled Caro, pretending to be an Indian brave, elbows and knees pumping up and down. The others followed her example, throwing back their heads and banging their hands against their lips.

"Your bum is shining as bright as the moon." Aoife was war dancing behind Jennifer.

"That's why it's called mooning," retorted Jennifer. "This is brilliant. I'm going to join a nudist colony when I'm older."

This statement produced sick-making sounds from the others. But, as Jennifer was always saying things to shock people, they did not really believe her. It was growing chilly. Although the beach was still wrapped in moonlight, a dusty glow was creeping over the sky. They made their way back to the rocks where they had carefully folded their clothes.

Not a stitch of clothing could be seen anywhere.

"Ahh!" they screamed, an outburst of horror that sent shivers of dread through each of them.

"This has to be the wrong rock," cried Caro, feverishly clambering on to the next one.

"It's not," whispered Aoife. "There's the Seven-Up bottle that we found in the rockpool. That's our landmark."

"What are we going to do?"

Jennifer, panic-stricken, dashed back from the rock where she had so casually slung her bra and panties. Her nudist colony ambitions had disappeared. So had her underwear. The night was full of unseen eyes, peering from behind every rock and sand dune. Humiliation. Mortification.

While Jennifer stayed under cover, her friends searched around, making clumsy clambering movements as they tried to keep their balance on the rocks.

"Whoever they are, they're probably watching us and laughing their heads off," moaned Aoife.

Seaweed squelched, a carpet of slime that was continually moving beneath their feet. The idea that the people from the beach party might be watching made them cringe. They were forced to report back to Jennifer empty-handed.

"What's that?" Something caught Caro's attention. Something white. She blinked, trying to adjust her eyes towards a flag-like object that was being waved from the entrance of Magpie Cave. It was not really a cave, just a long narrow tunnel, shaped naturally when the fall of rocks created a high roof and damp craggy walls. It was musty-smelling, littered with driftwood and tin cans. The tide swept so much rubbish into the tunnel that it resembled a magpie's nest. Hence its name.

"Shhhh!" Caro held up her hand for silence. "Someone's calling my name."

"Caro, Caro, come to me. I am the ghost of Cross Hollow. The soil is heavy on my chest!"

Jennifer was breathing heavily, a sound like that normally heard during a heart attack. Then, recognising her bra, she began to yell. She told her twin brothers what she thought of them, what she would do to them, and what she would like to do to them, slowly, without mercy, without end.

"I hope you'll put your clothes on first, White Bum." This disrespectful reply floated over from the cave. Jennifer moaned and sank to the ground, muttering quite unrepeatable things.

"That's worse than *The Commitments*!" gasped Aoife. "Where did you learn that kind of language?"

"It was a gift, given to me at birth by a good fairy who knew what living with five brothers would be like," cried Jennifer.

"David! Michael! Can we have our clothes back? Please!" begged Caro, knowing instinctively that this was a time for being humble. "We're very cold and wet and upset. It was a good joke but we want our clothes back now. Poor Jennifer is crying her heart out!"

"I am n—" Jennifer's mouth was firmly gagged by Aoife.

"Aw! Poor little White Bum." The mocking tones from Magpie Cave suggested that the twins did not believe one word of Caro's humble act. In fact it sounded as if they were choking to death with laughter.

"I hope they do," thought Caro, grimly, wondering how she could ever, for one moment, for one fraction of

71

a second, have imagined she fancied David Hilliard.

"Tell her to stop crying. Tell her we'll be very kind and return all her clothes. But only on certain conditions."

"Name your conditions," shouted Caro, knowing, from the slightly deeper pitch of the voice, that she was speaking to David. She vowed that she would never again notice any difference between the twins. Pure poison, both of them.

"Tell her she's to stop zapping the channels and dancing in front of the television set every time we try to watch football," David demanded.

"Agreed," said Caro, ignoring Jennifer, who was trying to break free from Aoife.

"Also we want our LP of REM returned and we want her to pay for the repair of our record player which she broke!"

Jennifer shook her head wildly. But Aoife's grip was strong.

"She *did* break it," hissed Emma. "I was with her when it happened. And she's hidden their REM album at the back of her wardrobe."

Caro cupped her hands around her mouth. "She agrees to everything. And she's very sorry for breaking your record player." This apology almost sent Jennifer's eyes shooting from their sockets. Her three friends stared sternly at her, defying her to utter one word of contradiction when Aoife removed her hand. The white bra was coming closer.

"They're going to see us!" The girls scattered, running for cover. But the twins stopped before rounding the rocks that sheltered the girls and laid four bundles of clothes on the sand.

"Go on. Take them. We'll turn our backs while you get

dressed," urged Michael.

Cautiously Caro edged from behind the rock. In her matching cropped top and panties, it had been decided that she was the most modestly dressed.

"Keep pretending it's a bikini," urged the others. "You run around the beach all the time in things skimpier than that and it doesn't bother you."

"That's different," said Caro, unable to explain why that should be the case, just knowing that it was. The twins were two identical grey blurs, their backs turned to Caro as they ran back to the cave. She sprinted towards the bundles of clothes. But she was reluctant to trust them an inch and wriggled into her jeans without taking off her wet underwear. Suddenly the idea of bed seemed wonderful. A warm duvet. Clean sheets, instead of sticky gritty clothes clinging to her damp skin. Even the idea of chasing the boys and burying them deep in sand with a tombstone of rocks, held no attraction for her. Dressed again and trying to restore some warmth to their bodies, the girls did on-the-spot jogging, flailing their arms and shaking their heads.

"We have to attack the cave," snarled Jennifer. "Honour has to be restored."

But the others had no energy left for revenge.

"If you won't come with me then I'm going in on my own," declared Jennifer, rolling up her sleeves. "I'm going to pulverise them into sand."

Her friends moaned but followed her towards Magpie Cave. They could not see anything in the blackness. Everyone jumped when Caro accidentally kicked a tin can and the sound clanged loudly.

"They *have* to be in here somewhere," insisted Jennifer, moving deeper into the centre of the tunnel.

"There's no one here. I'm not going in any further." Emma sounded fed up.

"I agree." She was joined by Aoife, the two girls gripping hands, stumbling together as they made their way back outside.

"Just wait!" Jennifer shouted, preparing to retreat. "You two dorks had better hire an army of bodyguards for the rest of your lives." The words bounced mockingly back at her.

At the entrance Jennifer spotted Michael trying to ease his way over the hump of rocks outside the cave. She yelled at Aoife and Emma. For the second time during the slumber party, the chase was on. Michael dropped down from the rocks on to the strand, sprinting towards the distant sand dunes where the grass would give him shelter. Caro was left behind, her heart skidding with shock when a pair of strong arms reached out from the darkness and grabbed her before she could move.

"It's only me, David. Stay here for a minute." His voice was behind her, close to her ear. The thump of her heart had nothing to do with the shock of his appearance. She struggled against him but his nearness, the feel of his breath against her neck was exciting, no matter how much she tried to deny it.

"This is the first time we've ever had a chance to be alone together." He moved in front of her. She still could not see him clearly, only the blurred image of his close-cropped hair with the long fringe, his head tilted to one side, watching her.

"David Hilliard. You're a pig. Stealing our clothes! How could you do such a disgusting thing?" she demanded.

"If you lived with Jennifer you'd know why," he

replied, not sounding in the least bit apologetic.

"And you've ruined my slumber party. Coming to my window like that. It's all you and your stupid brother's fault that we're locked out." She took a step away from him and felt the surface of the rock against her back. "I'll be in big trouble if my parents find out where I've been."

"But they need never know because I have come to your rescue." He squeezed his hand into the back pocket of his jeans, then, holding his hand close to her face, jangled her keys.

"My keys! Where did you get them?" Caro demanded.

"I found them after you dropped them. But I was holding on to them, just to see what you'd do. Then when I went to give them back to you, you and those other loopers were climbing into Hobourne Park. We followed you, just to see what you were going to do."

"Very funny. Ha Ha Ha!" She snatched her key-ring from him.

"We saw you doing your Peeping Tom act on that poor guy in his car. You sure got some music going down on The Slopes." He began to laugh at the memory of the car procession and the panic the girls had created.

"You can't talk about Peeping Toms," retorted Caro. "You and your brother were spying on us when we were swimming."

"I know," he sighed, sadly. "It was just our luck that the only time we get to see a naked girl it has to be our sister."

"Oh you!" Caro slapped him across the side of his head, trying not to giggle. "You're going to be in real trouble when she catches up with you."

"I'd better make the best of it then," he said, moving closer. The rock was a cocoon, sheltering them from the world outside. If he kissed her no one would see, no one would know. A private moment in a mad night. There were soft hairs on his upper lip, sand on his face. It felt gritty against her cheek and she knew that he would taste the sea when he touched her lips. It was only the briefest of kisses. Her first kiss. In that instant it broke the shyness she always felt towards him. Her shoulders relaxed. She wondered if a second kiss would be as exciting. But there was no time to find out. The shrieks of the girls grew louder. Second kisses, decided Caro, would have to wait for another time.

They pulled apart and moved from the shelter of the cave entrance, their eyes trying to pierce the gloom. Faint red-tipped spears of light warmed the sky in the east but overhead it was still dark with clouds banking over the sea like blue-black mountains. Michael was slung in a hammock shape between the three girls, desperately trying to escape from them as they staggered towards the water.

"Oh my God! They're going to drown him!" yelled David, preparing to run to his assistance but tripping over Caro's foot, which happened, conveniently, to be in his way.

"Have you no shame, Miss Kane?" he demanded, sprawling on the sand. "One minute you're kissing me and the next minute you're trying to handicap me."

"No shame at all, Mr Hilliard," she replied.

But her laughter stopped suddenly when she saw two pinpoints of light in the distance. Car lights. Passion killers. Discovery. The same thoughts were also flashing through the minds of the girls who had been on the point of slinging Michael into the water. They dropped him on the wet sand and sprinted towards the cave. Michael jumped to his feet and followed.

The garda car had a spotlight on the roof, a siren, and two spinning blue lights. It filled the teenagers with terror as it raced along the hardpacked sand. The pitch black of the cave was not as frightening as the whining siren and searching lights. They held hands, stumbled and bumped against each other in the inky dark. The noise grew louder. It echoed inside the cave, reverberating from the rocky walls. Then suddenly the clamour stopped. The silence was like a blanket, heavy, falling over everyone to their great relief. A relief that was short-lived for when Caro peeped out, the garda car had parked right in front of Magpie Cave. As a burly figure stepped out, she recognised the loud voice of Sergeant Hilliard.

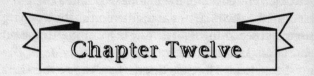

Chapter Twelve

"**Y**our dad! It's your dad!" She imagined that a death rattle would sound something similar to the croak in her voice. David, who had supported her when she fell back into the cave, almost let her drop.

"You're having me on!"

"No. I heard him. Listen."

Six bodies tensed, shuddered, pinched themselves in the hope that it was a bad dream. No such luck. Caro edged back towards the entrance. In the headlights she could make out the broad outline of Sergeant Hilliard staring at the sea. The two car doors were open. The sergeant coughed loudly.

"Must you smoke those cancer sticks in my company, O'Hara?"

"Sorry Sergeant. Just one. I'm gasping for a smoke." The smell of cigarette smoke wafted into the cave.

"I'm glad to see that my morality campaign is having some effect." There was no mistaking the brisk, self-satisfied voice. "Apart from that crowd of thugs and their beach party, The Slopes were very quiet tonight. As was Hobourne Park."

"Apart from Mrs Boggan." Garda O'Hara was from Donegal and sounded like Daniel O'Donnell.

"Well...ahem...that was most unfortunate. How were we supposed to know that she went ghost-hunting at this unearthly hour. Especially with a man."

"You mean Professor Price, President of the Celtic Seekers After Psychic Knowledge, who is currently giving a series of lectures to a number of Irish psychic societies?" queried Garda O'Hara. Caro had the distinct impression that he was trying not to laugh.

"Hump." Sergeant Hilliard cleared his throat. "Most unfortunate. You'll have to apologise to the lady in the morning."

"Me! I had nothing to do with it. I wasn't the one who twisted the professor's arm behind his back and demanded identification."

"I was standing behind the man, O'Hara. He was in shadow. How was I to realise his age?"

"He did try and explain what he was doing, Sergeant. But I suppose you were too busy body-searching him to understand what he was saying."

"Listen, O'Hara, that's enough talk out of you, now. You call to Mrs Boggan in the morning and tender the apologies of the Beachwood Gardaí. Let that be the end of the matter," snapped Sergeant Hilliard.

"I thought Mrs Boggan was very unfair when she called you a threat to the environment. How did she put it? 'Your mind was like a polluted river, filled with the slurry of an over-active imagination.'"

"Garda O'Hara! Have you ever considered the possibility of a transfer to Rockall Island?" asked Sergeant

Hilliard.

"But that's just an uninhabited rock, Sergeant."

"That's exactly what I was thinking. The perfect place for you. Then you can gab away all you like to the seagulls."

Garda O'Hara fell silent.

The three Hilliards had gone into a state of shock, their bodies flattened against the walls, hoping to turn themselves into rock until after their father left. He seemed in no hurry to oblige.

Garda O'Hara drew deeply on his cigarette, scattering ash and blowing smoke rings.

"Disgusting habit." Sergeant Hilliard flapped his hand before his face. "You young people have no self-control."

"I tried six times to give them up, Sergeant."

"That's what I mean. No staying power. No discipline. You should see some of the carry-on of the youngsters I come across. No shame. No decency. And the girls are every bit as bad as the boys."

"But weren't you young once yourself, Sergeant?"

"In my day it was different. None of this staying up until all hours. And spending the day lounging in front of the television set. Have you noticed the eyes of today's young people? Square! As for the clothes the girls wear! Disgusting. What do they call those black things? Body suits? Huh. I've seen black puddings wearing looser skins. I blame the parents, O'Hara. You see a young person who's misbehaving and I'll show you a bad parent."

"But, they're not all like that, Sergeant," Garda O'Hara had obviously heard this lecture many times and was very bored with it.

"That's right, O'Hara. Some parents do indeed know

how to bring up their children. Take my six for instance. I don't want to boast but I have to say this. From the beginning I laid down certain ground rules in my house. They are allowed to watch only the television programmes that I find suitable. None of this satellite junk. They have to study for four hours every evening and six hours at the weekend. If they do not eat what is served up to them, then it is served up to them again at the next meal. As for staying up late! I only have to say the word 'bed' and they go immediately."

There was a faint slumping sound beside Caro. She suspected that one of the Hilliard twins had fainted. Tough luck. The Hilliards had haunted and ruined her slumber party. And I'm now being forced to listen to their father's rubbish, she thought, furiously.

She knew that Jennifer had a system for smuggling her leftover food out of the house and feeding it to Rachmaninov. Mrs Kane often threatened to put a lock on her fridge before Jennifer arrived because it was always empty after she left. As for television! Telly addict was her middle name. When she was in Caro's house she sat in front of the set, never taking her eyes off the screen even during the advertisements. Sergeant Hilliard was so full of self-importance that he never once considered the possibility of his children disobeying him. Since Jennifer's thirteenth birthday she had escaped from her bedroom on six occasions when she was supposed to be studying and gone down to Fountain Square, where the young people of Beachwood hung out. Nor did their father know that the twins had started smoking when they were twelve and given it up on their fourteenth birthday. Caro had seen them sitting beside their open bedroom window blowing smoke out into the back garden. He refused to allow rock music to be played in the house and would have been astonished to know that his son Gerry was anxious to form a rock group and play drums with her brother, Danny. They were going to call themselves Dancing on Grey Ash. Sergeant Hilliard's eldest son, Brian, was trying to work up courage to tell his father that he wanted to drop out of sixth year and become a disc jockey on local radio. Jennifer's younger brother, Fergal, who was only eleven, was going out with a girl two years older than him.

Sergeant Hilliard was a silly pompous man but he was also a powerful one. He only had to walk a few paces into the cave and they would be discovered. Sheer nerves made Caro want to giggle. Emma and Aoife were beside her and she knew, oh how she knew, that they felt the same way. Tears in their eyes, insides heaving, knuckles clenched to their mouths to prevent the sound escaping. It always happened at the most awful times. At PE when Miss Cullen's bust heaved up and down during on-the-spot jogging or when Mrs Brennan sang opera to the class and her tonsils could be seen. Sometimes it even happened when Fr Cowan was delivering the Sunday sermon and they would be thumped on the shoulders by cross-looking women and ordered to leave the church. Put quite simply—giggling fits happened whenever they shouldn't happen and once started, were impossible to control.

"Don't dare to giggle." Jennifer knew the signs, could hear the spluttering gasps. "He'll hear you."

Splutter..splutter..splutter.

"Shut up!"

"Can't!"

Shoulders shaking. Mouths clenched rigid. Whimpers still managing to escape.

"What's that noise, Sergeant? It came from the cave. I'd better investigate."

The probing beam of a torch. Giggles choked into silence. They held their breath, as silent as the rocks surrounding them. A shadow loomed in the centre beam of light, hesitated, reluctant to venture into the musty-smelling tunnel.

"I wouldn't worry about that noise, O'Hara. I'm sure it's a rat. The place is infested with them."

"You're probably right, Sergeant." The torch clicked off.

Rats! Caro's legs began to itch. She could imagine a damp, shiny nose probing beneath the hem of her jeans. Tiny sharp claws sinking into her ankles, using her leg as a ladder. Ugh! She would scream. Go hysterical. Dance madly on the floor of Magpie Cave and scatter the armies of rats that were crawling closer.

"Don't scream," warned Jennifer. "My father's hearing is as keen as a bat's."

Bats! They lived in caves. Blind eyes. Tissue-paper wings tangling in her hair. Greedy lips sucking the life blood from her veins. Oh how she hated the Hilliards. How could she have kissed David Hilliard in this rat- and bat-infested cave? How could she have danced behind Jennifer Hilliard's naked bum and thought it was the funniest thing in the world? How could she have left her comfortable house and become involved in this madcap adventure that was going to end in death by rat- or bat-poisoning.

Sergeant Hilliard, thankfully unaware of her agony, continued to drone on. "As for those young thugs who were running loose around this place tonight. Did you see the cheeky look on their faces when I ordered them off home?"

"They were just young people having a beach party, Sergeant. They weren't doing any harm."

"Drinking beer and smoking God knows what! As for those songs. Call that music? I'd play a better melody if I danced on saucepans. I can't imagine what sort of parents would allow their children out until that hour."

"They weren't children. They were adults."

"You're a young man, O'Hara, but you'll have your own family some day. I'm telling you now, lay down the ground rules and the rest will fall into place. Unlike the parents of those young thugs, I know where each of my children is at this moment in time."

Sergeant Hilliard sighed with satisfaction and checked his watch. "Throw away that cancer stick, O'Hara. It's time we were leaving. We'll do one more round of Hobourne Park then go back to the station." The engine purred into life, the car moved out of sight.

Six young people shot out from Magpie Cave as if they had just been ejected from a cannon. They were a strange sight, shaking their arms, stamping their feet, running their hands frantically through their hair. No rats or bats emerged. After a few minutes the hysteria died away. They sank, exhausted, on the sand.

"A model family!" growled Aoife. "Now I've heard *everything*."

"Unlike the parents of those young thugs I know where each of my children is at this moment in time." Caro mimicked Sergeant Hilliard's loud, smug voice. "So do I, Sergeant. So do I!"

"Oh, stop it." Jennifer was not one bit amused. There was no mischief in her eyes now, only anxiety. "We'd better get going. We can all start thinking about emigration if he finds us."

"But supposing he sees us going through Hobourne Park or the village?" fretted Michael.

"There's only one thing to do," declared David. "We'll have to go through Twist and Shout. No one ever goes there and it'll bring us out at the car park beside the back entrance."

"Oh no!" moaned Emma. "What if we meet the ghost of Cross Hollow?"

"You *can't* believe in that rubbish!" David scoffed.

"It's true," protested Aoife, reluctant to have her most recent story discredited.

"No, it's not." David was not taking any nonsense from them. "Look, it's the only sensible idea."

"But we might see Norton Hobourne's head," moaned Caro.

"Would you prefer to see my father's head?" David reminded her.

Caro shuddered.

"Don't worry. I'll protect you, frightened child," he said, putting his arms around her, cuddling her into him.

"Push off, pest," she struggled free. Her friends were not going to know anything about what had happened in the cave. They would never stop teasing her. She ran down the beach, trying to force bravado into her voice. "Let's go, gang. We've got a date with a ghost!"

Chapter Thirteen

A s the group left Beachwood Strand, a mist shielded the hazy sunrise. But as soon as they entered the woods, this early morning light was dulled by tree trunks growing closely together. Thin saplings tangled with briars and chopped tree stumps. Moss and ivy, the smell of musty decaying leaves, rustling sounds underfoot, the snap of dead wood, added to their terror. Now and then flickers of light shone through the thick foliage where birds, hidden but alert, watched their progress, sleepily shrilling out their disapproval. For one heart-stopping moment Caro thought she would faint when something swooped out of the gloom and glided silently over her head. This was Twist and Shake, fertile ground for horror stories, for seeing the ghost of Cross Hollow, for losing one's way.

"We're lost," declared Caro.

"We couldn't be." It was the third time David had denied this fact.

"We passed this way a few minutes ago. We're just

circling the same trail."

"She's right." Michael pointed to the edge of the trail. Litter always drifted into Twist and Shake. Bleached newspapers and ice-pop wrappers had become embedded on thorny briars. "We passed that lot already."

The three of them had been walking behind the girls, not noticing that they were gradually drawing ahead. Anyone walking with Emma always had to walk fast to keep up with her long stride. Caro and the twins had been discussing the latest LP from REM. She was pleased to discover that they shared her taste in music, loved the same groups, The 4 Of Us, Rozalla, The Shamen and The Fat Lady Sings. It took some time to realise that they were walking in circles.

Twist and Shake was full of narrow trails. In daylight, there were certain landmarks to guide them in the right direction. But in the dim shadowy light, everything looked the same. They stopped, glancing helplessly around.

"I think we turn off this way," said Michael.

"No, keep on this trail. We're going the right way," said David.

"It's straight ahead," said Caro.

"There's nothing like a united opinion to solve problems." Michael turned to the right, glancing back at the other two. They shrugged and followed him.

Oh! This endless night. Caro was exhausted. Her cropped top and panties were still damp, the panties tight against her bottom. If only she could give them a pull and loosen them. But she would die of discomfort rather than let the twins see her doing anything like that. She was cold and shivery. To think that she had tidied her room so carefully, had spent her precious pocket money on joss sticks. Pancake batter was waiting in the fridge to be sizzled in a hot pan. Her mouth watered at the thought. Caster sugar and lemon juice, melted butter running down her chin. She must stop thinking like that or she would go crazy.

The dawn mist had deepened, flitting between the trees like a will-o'-the-wisp. In some patches the air was clear. Then, an instant later, they would have to feel their way through a dense cloud.

Suddenly her skin rippled with fear. She had seen something through the trees. Something that moved. A sharp gust of wind blew the leaves and disturbed the mist. She could see it, staring down at them from the branches of the tree overhead. It was not a bird. Sometimes grey squirrels could be seen in the park, scurrying up tree trunks. But this was no squirrel.

"What is it?" Her hand trembled so much she could barely raise it. Eyes were staring down at them. Luminous eyes, filled with evil. Lips, red and gleaming, stretched in a hideous smile. It was a head without a body. Lord Norton Hobourne. There was no mistaking the features of the face. Deep lines around the mouth, straggly black hair falling over a wrinkled forehead. A depraved face. The face of a man who would murder young girls and bury their bodies in the dead of night.

"Lo...Lo...Lord Ho...Ho!"

"It's Lord Hobourne!" breathed David, finishing her stuttered sentence. "Let's get out of here! Fast!"

They dodged between the trees, leaving the trail, feeling their feet sinking into soft, springy moss. When Caro looked back she could only see dark shapes. Tree trunks and leaves, bending branches hiding the gruesome head. But she knew it was following them. In the morning their bodies would be found, dead and cold as ice.

A glimmer of light shone through the trees. Frantic, panting, they ran towards it. The trees thinned and opened out into a dense mist that buried every familiar landmark from sight. They peered through the mist, beginning to make out blurred outlines. A high wire fence. They had not arrived in Hobourne car park but had gone in the opposite direction. Caro knew this place. They were standing on the lip of Cross Hollow. Mist hung over the valley like a sheet of heaped snow.

"Oh my God!" David moaned, staring in horror at the scene below them, at the shapes shimmering through the mist. White crosses. In neat rows they stood, perfectly still, telling the story of Lord Norton Hobourne's cruel deeds. He towered above them, headless, arms stretched out in a vain attempt to find his lost head.

Like a sigh a gentle breeze drifted over him. The mist seemed to waver, the crosses bent, fluttered, as if reaching towards the three young people.

"She was right. Aoife was telling the tr—" With a low moan Michael slumped at her feet. David took one horrified look at his twin and followed his example.

"Help!" screamed Caro. "Someone help me."

She covered her face with her hands, begging her body to faint. But her heart continued to pump, her hands to sweat, her throat to scream and her mind to cope with the knowledge that countless ghosts were watching her beyond the mist. When she stopped screaming she heard footsteps. Jennifer dashed into the opening, followed by her two friends.

"What's wrong? You've scared us to death. We've been searching for you for ages. Have my brothers been trying to get off with you?"

"I've seen him," sobbed Caro. "The ghost of Cross Hollow and all his murdered wives are down there, hiding under the crosses, and David and Michael are dead." She sobbed more loudly. Jennifer, Aoife and Emma took one look into the valley, screamed and ran back into Twist and Shake, tripping over Michael as they went.

"No! No! Come back! His head's in there. Up a tree. Come back! Come back!"

Emma, Aoife and Jennifer, still screaming, plunged back out of the woods.

"It was a true story, locked in my subconscious mind." Aoife's voice cracked with amazement.

David opened his eyes. His skin was the colour of a plucked and frozen chicken. Discovering that the girls had no intention of reviving him, he pulled himself into a sitting position with his back propped against the fence, then bent his head between his knees. Two figures emerged from the trees, causing a fresh outburst of screaming. This final blast of sound brought Michael back to the land of the conscious.

"Dear, dear, dear! What a commotion," said a voice. "I'm afraid, Professor Price, that you are not going to hear a banshee keening tonight. That most unearthly sound seems to have a definite earthly keen to it." Mrs Boggan was wearing green wellingtons and carried a tape recorder with a cord draped around her neck. A microphone was in her hand, directed towards the girls whose screams had died away. The small man beside her was swinging a blackthorn walking stick. His head was dome-shaped, as bald as an egg. Professor Price shook his head in disappointment. "My word, that was some cacophony. A real hullabaloo."

Caro pointed into a valley. "The ghost of Cross Hollow. He's down there with all his murdered wives."

Professor Price looked totally bewildered. "Is this an Irish myth, Mrs Boggan? I was unaware that the ghost of Cross Hollow had more than one wife. Where on earth are these ghostly spirits?"

"Under the white crosses," sobbed Emma.

Mrs Boggan stared down into the valley. The breeze was lifting the mist, thinning it in places. "I think she's referring to the market garden, Professor. Look closely and you'll see what she means." To hear Mrs Boggan chuckling in the middle of such supernatural horrors astonished the young people.

"Oh yes. I see now." Professor Price smiled.

Mrs Boggan turned Caro around until she was facing the valley. "Don't you know what those white crosses are, my dears? I was only speaking to Mr Tobin, the owner of the garden centre, yesterday and he told me he had cut white plastic bags into strips and placed them crossways on frames to scare the birds off his cabbage plants. As an added protection, he erected the scarecrow, Giant Haystacks, to wrestle with any bird brave enough to take him on. I'm afraid we are not going to see the ghost of Cross Hollow tonight, or his wives, whoever they may be."

When the young people stared down into the valley it was impossible to mistake the white crosses for anything other than thin strips of fluttering criss-crossed plastic, overlooked by Giant Haystacks. They had often seen similar tricks used to scare off hungry birds. Mr Kane used yellow rags on his vegetable patch. Michael slumped against the fence, as energetic as a rag doll that has lost its stuffing.

"Ghosts! Ghosts!" he kept muttering. "We saw the ghost of Lord Hobourne's head staring down at us."

Mrs Boggan smiled at the professor. "I think I can also explain the origins of that gruesome object," she said. "As you know, my dears, I am addicted to junk food and Patrick the Pizza Prince is a regular caller to my home. So I recognised the head when it stared down at me from the tree and the professor was most intrigued by the luminous glow it cast."

"Oh no!" gasped Caro, covering her face with her hands. "It's the Pizza Poltergeist." The blush began at the tips of her toes and ended at the top of her head.

"I'm afraid reality can take on some strange disguises in the half-light of dawn, as you have discovered. Which brings me to a very serious question. What on earth are you young people doing out at such an hour? Do slumber parties involve running around public parks so early?" A disapproving note had crept into Mrs Boggan's voice.

"They don't," admitted Caro. "But we've had an awful time. You wouldn't believe all the things that have happened to us."

"Try us," said the elderly man.

"You're the ghost-hunter." Aoife was thrilled to be in the company of such a famous person. She searched her pockets for a scrap of paper but, finding none, stretched her leg out in front of his astonished eyes. "I haven't got my autograph book with me, Professor. So could you sign the leg of my jeans instead?"

"Is this another strange Irish custom?" the professor asked, taking a pen from his jacket pocket.

"Needs must do," said Mrs Boggan. She was not smiling. "I'm waiting for your explanation, everyone."

When the girls had finished their tale of woe, Professor

Price patted Caro's hand.

"Sergeant Hilliard is a very busy man indeed." He sounded grim. "And I can well understand your reluctance to avoid being seen by him. But really, you should all be in your beds."

"I agree!" said Mrs Boggan. "Go straight home, all of you, and we'll say no more about it."

"We'd better return to collect my camera," said the professor. "I had just rested it on that tree stump when we heard the girls screaming."

"We'll find it easily enough, Professor. I know exactly where you left it." Mrs Boggan flapped her hands at the young people. "Go on! We're too old to try and keep up with young limbs. Start walking. And no more mischief. Follow the trail to the right and it will bring you into the car park."

The professor waved his blackthorn stick at them in farewell then followed Mrs Boggan through the trees. For a while no one spoke. Then Caro turned to the girls. "You're some friends," she sniffed. "Running off and leaving me with two corpses on my hands."

"I wasn't fooled by those crosses for a minute," declared Jennifer. "I was just putting on the act."

"Me too," lied Emma.

The boys, looking as sick as parrots, said nothing.

"I never realised that my imagination had so much effect on you." Aoife began to laugh. The others glared at her. None of them believed they would ever be able to forgive her.

When they reached the tree of horror, the Pizza Poltergeist was still staring down at them. David swung himself up on to the low branches in an effort to recover some of his self-esteem. He pulled the Pizza Poltergeist free and placed it over his face, leering eerily down at them.

"Hey Batman. Mind you don't faint," mocked his sister. She was obviously going to enjoy herself in the days ahead.

"That's a souvenir of tonight." David jumped down, ignored his sister and handed the carton to Caro.

"I don't think I want to remember anything about tonight," sighed Caro, tucking it under her arm.

"As long as you remember one thing," he grinned and touched her lip with his finger.

The trail had widened.

"Pancakes!" said Caro.

"Let's race," said Emma.

She started running. The others followed, anxious to leave the secrets of Twist and Shake behind them. Together they sprinted towards the mist beyond the trees. Sprinted into the pebbled surface of Hobourne car park where the mist was dense and muffled the sound of their footsteps. Sprinted into the headlights and the waiting arms of Sergeant Hilliard and Garda O'Hara.

Chapter Fourteen

"**H**old it right there!"

Strong arms grabbed the twins. Caro and Jennifer were pinned to Garda O'Hara's chest.

"Against the car. Immediately!" shouted Sergeant Hilliard. "You thugs may think you can run like wild savages around a public park. Well, I'm about to tell you differently. Face that car and spread your legs. Hands on the roof."

In the open space of the car park, the density of the mist shielded the sergeant's face. With the blue light flashing he looked as fearsome as Lord Norton Hobourne and all his ghostly wives. The whole episode had happened so quickly that he had not yet glimpsed the faces of his sons. Or his daughter. Just blurred terrified figures, hands over their eyes as the headlights beamed into the mist and distorted the scene into one that could only belong to hell. Emma poised, ready to flee. The swiftest race of her life so far.

"I said everybody!" shouted Sergeant Hilliard. "And

that includes you!"

They turned and faced the garda car. The roof was damp with dew, cold steel under their fingers. Three on each side they stood, watching their past lives flashing before their eyes.

"I want to die," whispered Jennifer. "It's the only solution."

Caro agreed. "I know what epitaph I want on my grave," she hissed. "I want them to write *I Hate the Hilliards*!"

"Give those thugs a body-search," ordered Sergeant Hilliard. "See if they're carrying drugs, tablets, solvents, alcohol, weapons or stolen goods. That will do for starters."

"Sergeant. They're girls," said Garda O'Hara, having discovered this unmistakable fact after his hand accidentally grabbed Jennifer's right breast when she tried to wriggle away from him.

"Girls?" Sergeant Hilliard roared, as if unable to understand the meaning of the word. "What is happening to this world of sorrow? Put them in the police car, Garda O'Hara. And radio for another car to bring these fine examples of manhood to the station. Not a muscle between them. It will be interesting to see what their parents have to say about this disgraceful episode."

Jennifer moaned softly.

"Silence!" snapped her father. "You've done enough screaming and hollering for one night. I'd like to know what you were doing in Hobourne Woods when you should have been in your beds like all decent people?"

The boys stiffened when their father began to pat their bodies with expert hands.

"You'd better talk fast, boys. What were you doing? Cider drinking? Drugs? Sex? I'm up to all your sleazy behaviour. I want the truth and I want it now. Do you understand the drift of my language?"

"Yes, Dad," gulped David.

"Don't be smart with me, you lazy good-for-nothing lout. If I was your father I'd know how to deal with you. Let me show you." He swung David around until his son was facing him.

"David!"

"Yeah, Dad. That's me."

Sergeant Hilliard roared. Caro, in the back seat of the police car, clapped her hands over her ears. Jennifer hid her face in her friend's lap. Sergeant Hilliard uttered another awesome roar when Michael turned around.

"Dear Lord above! If you are looking down on me tonight, please tell me that my eyes are deceiving me. I *order* you to tell me that my eyes are deceiving me."

"I'm afraid he can't, Dad," admitted Michael.

Convicted criminals on death row had more hope in their voices. The twins shivered, looking helplessly at the man in front of them. He opened the car door and stared at Caro.

"Caroline Kane! I cannot believe this. And who is that young lady with her face in your lap? If you mention the name Hilliard, I will imprison you for life."

"Hi, Dad." Jennifer lifted her head and tried to smile at her father. "We can explain everything."

"Are these your children, Sergeant?" Garda O'Hara sounded very interested. "What an unexpected surprise! I've heard so much about them. But I never imagined we'd meet under such circumstances. By the way Sergeant, do you still want me to radio for that second car?"

Sergeant Hilliard stared at him with loathing.

"Ahem. Hrumph. Go into the woods, O'Hara, and

check if there are any other delinquents about."

"I'm sure you've arrested them all."

"Do as I say," snapped the sergeant.

As soon as Garda O'Hara had disappeared through the trees, Sergeant Hilliard ordered the girls out of the car and lined the six young people up in front of him. "I called you thugs before I realised your identity. I now see no reason to change my mode of address." He laced his fingers together, cracking his knuckles.

Caro wished that she was back in the wood again, staring up into the ghostly features of Lord Norton Hobourne.

"Do you realise that I have just made a laughing stock of myself in front of a subordinate. By tomorrow this story will be known to the entire Beachwood police force. By the following day, it will be told in every garda station in Dublin. Soon it will be nationwide. So I am hoping that one of you has a reasonable explanation because we are talking about serious grounding here. It's known as life imprisonment with the key thrown away. Start talking."

Six faces stared at the ground. A tear dripped from Caro's eye and landed on the toe of her Doc Martens. Another followed.

"No sign of any young people," called out Garda O'Hara on his return. "But I'm afraid we've disturbed Mrs Boggan and Professor Price again."

"My word. Another commotion. We'll have a mass exodus of ghostly spirits from Cross Hollow if this continues," exclaimed Professor Price. "I keep believing I am hearing supernatural howlings. But each time it turns out to have an earthly source."

"I've told them about hearing these young people in

the woodlands," explained Garda O'Hara.

"It's been quite a busy night for the Beachwood gardaí," said Mrs Boggan. She sounded extremely snooty and annoyed. "Disturbing innocent ghost-hunters, not to mention the stress this causes the ghost of Cross Hollow who will only appear under calm conditions. And now you have arrested our helpers."

"Your helpers!" Sergeant Hilliard gasped. "Your helpers!"

"Yes indeed, Sergeant. They are the junior branch of the Beachwood Celtic Seekers After Psychic Knowledge and were kind enough to give up their night's sleep to help Professor Price and myself in our ghost of Cross Hollow project. They have taken some very useful notes for us and we have also recorded their observations."

"It's a wonder your mother didn't mention this to me when I spoke to her on the phone, Caroline," Sergeant Hilliard snapped, looking keenly at Caro.

"She...uh...em..." Please dear God, I swear I will never sin again if you will only get me out of this one. Caro had never prayed with such silent devotion.

"Mrs Kane would not have known about it at that stage," Mrs Boggan interrupted. "We arranged this project only late in the evening when Professor Price expressed an interest in viewing the area haunted by the ghost of Cross Hollow. We planned to keep a vigil to see if the apparition should appear. But, as soon as these junior members became aware of our quest, they very kindly offered us their assistance."

"Why didn't you tell me you were going to do this?" The sergeant shook a finger at his children. His manner was beginning to mellow.

"We...well...we thought you wouldn't allow us to go

on the project," replied David.

"So why should I refuse permission for something as worthy as that?" demanded their father. He sounded like the most reasonable man in the world.

"Because you normally do," muttered Michael. "I mean you care a lot about our night's sleep and knowing where we are and...and...all that sort of thing..."

"And you'd gone on night duty by then, Dad," Jennifer interrupted. "We didn't want to disturb you with trivial requests. We know how important your job is and how much responsibility you have to cope with." The honeyed tone in Jennifer's voice made Caro cringe. If she used that tactic on her father, he usually said, "Cut it out girl and just tell me how much lighter my wallet will be after you leave."

Sergeant Hilliard tried not to look too pleased. "Be that as it may, it still does not explain why you were screaming like banshees. I'm sure you could be heard a mile away."

"We were giving Professor Price a demonstration of Irish folklore," explained Aoife. "He had no idea how a banshee's keen sounded."

"It was most impressive," agreed Professor Price. "If I had any hair it would have stood on end."

"Wait a minute!" Sergeant Hilliard was becoming suspicious again. "How come I didn't notice them when I met you earlier in Hobourne Castle?"

"When you interrupted our research in the ruins of Hobourne Castle, these young people were searching for a ring which one of them had dropped. Fortunately, they found it and were then able to continue with their night's work," explained Mrs Boggan.

Caro wondered, as she often did, how grown-ups

managed to tell the truth when they were actually telling a lie.

"Unfortunately Professor Price has not yet recovered from the rough treatment you inflicted upon him." Mrs Boggan paused, holding up her tape recorder. "At the time we had hoped to record psychic movements within the haunted area and play it back at our next branch meeting. But instead we recorded the entire incident and the comments you made. I wonder what our members will make of that."

Sergeant Hilliard cleared his throat in an utterly miserable cough. "Yes, well, that was a most unfortunate error of judgement."

"I certainly agree with you on that point, Sergeant Hilliard. I feel that the least said to anyone about this night, the better. After all, Professor Price is a most respected man in his field of study. It would be very distressing if that unfortunate incident became public knowledge. The reputation of Irish hospitality is at stake here."

"Too true, Mrs Boggan, too true." Sergeant Hilliard's head bowed in humble apology.

"Perhaps I should put this tape into a safe place and, like the rest of us, it will stay mute on the subject. I don't imagine our little group would be all that interested in hearing what went on in Hobourne Castle. What do you think, Sergeant Hilliard?"

"I think that's an excellent idea, Mrs Boggan." His relief was mixed with a strong suspicion that Mrs Boggan was playing him like a fish on a hook. But the sight of the tape, clasped firmly in her hand, silenced his doubts.

"Goodnight, Sergeant. I'm sure you have more important things to do with your time than to stand around talking. Don't worry about the junior branch of the Celtic Seekers After Psychic Knowledge. We'll escort them safely to their homes," said Mrs Boggan.

"Come on, you lot. Lift those knees and start marching," ordered Professor Price.

Carefully avoiding their father's eyes, the twins and Jennifer fell into step in front of Professor Price. Garda O'Hara looked very dejected as he watched them march into the mist, pictures of virtue, doers of good deeds, keepers of secrets. "Nice family, Sergeant," he said.

"Hmmm!" replied his superior. "I wonder. I just wonder about that!"

As she walked across Oaktree Green Caro wondered how Mrs Boggan and Professor Price would feel if she fell on her knees and kissed their hands, their feet, the ground they walked upon.

But Professor Price disturbed her train of thought. He was gazing intently at the back of Jennifer's head as she marched in front of him.

"I couldn't help noticing the outside of your house, Mrs Boggan. It's badly in need of a good coat of paint."

"Indeed it is," she replied, sighing. "But I'm getting old. I could do with a new pair of hands."

There was a slight pause.

"We'll do it, Mrs Boggan," offered the twins.

"That's very kind of you," said Professor Price. "I also noticed the weeds. Such weeds! One could get lost in that garden, even with a compass."

"It's my poor back," explained Mrs Boggan. "It's not what it used to be."

"I'll do it," said Caro and Aoife together.

"This is too much," exclaimed the old woman. "Such charity from ones so young. It makes me believe in the goodness of today's youth despite Sergeant Hilliard's nasty morality campaign."

"I reckon a month should see your house in ship-shape order again," said the professor. "On my next visit, I shall look forward to a complete transformation. Shall I be disappointed?" he asked.

"No, Professor Price. You won't!" The resigned chorus came from six young people who knew that they had aged one hundred years in the last hour. They had never believed that grown-ups could be so devious.

"Goodnight, my dears." The two elderly people waited until the young people had disappeared into their homes.

"You devil," chuckled Mrs Boggan. "Talk about emotional blackmail!"

"Everything in life has a price," replied the professor. "Even slumber parties."

"Oh, to be young again," sighed Mrs Boggan. "I never believed slumber parties could be so interesting."

"Come now, Miranda." Professor Price linked her arm. "We were having our own little party in Hobourne Castle when that dreadful sergeant interrupted us."

"Yes indeed, we were." She sighed happily.

"So let us away to Spirit's Rest. Remember Miranda, I have yet to hear a real live Irish banshee keen."

"So you shall, my dear. So you shall."

The mist swirled, hiding them from view. But their laughter lingered in the quiet dawn that rested over Beachwood Village.

Other Beachwood Titles

The Debs Ball

School Bully

Summer at Fountain Square